THE TOWN THAT FEARED DUSK

Books by Calvin Demmer

Short Story Collections
The Sea Was a Fair Master
Dark Celebrations
The Town That Feared Dusk
Her Heart Beats for Ancient Beasts
Through the Ravenous Night We Ride
Duel the Darkness for Nightmare Rule

THE TOWN THAT FEARED DUSK

CALVIN DEMMER

TABLE OF CONTENTS

WELCOME TO GOOHILL 7

THE BRIDGE THAT SHOULD NOT BE 17

A GIFT FROM THE BRIDGE 27

THE HOUSE THAT REMAINED 35

SHOWDOWN AT THE LIBRARY 43

THE TOWN THAT FEARED DUSK 55

A DINER AT THE END OF THE WORLD 77

FROM DUSK TILL DEATH 95

NOW LEAVING GOOHILL....................................... 111

WELCOME TO GOOHILL

"You'll never have all the answers to the mystery that is Goohill. That's what makes it beautiful and unique." Ivan Reed cleared his throat. "Sure, there are a few people who tried to piece it all together. And hell, some even came close. I know I have. But, if the town's own librarian can't even solve all the mysteries, what chance do you have?"

Laura sighed.

"But then again, who can trust that odd woman? Maybe she wants the secrets all for herself." Ivan looked at the plate in front of him. The sandwich and fries he had consumed were gone, except for some lettuce, a few crumbs, and a healthy pool of ketchup. "I've snooped around quite a bit. I just can't seem to find a gap for a proper search, you know?"

Laura nodded.

She had headed to the diner straight after school. Her friend Bill had assured her that Ivan had a way for her to enter the back rooms of the library, where old town papers and books were stored. Unfortunately, Ivan was a peculiar old man and liked to ramble before getting to business. She had a decision to make: be kind and listen further or get to the point.

"Now let me tell you how I came to get this key," Ivan said, tapping his shirt pocket. "The obtaining of this key is quite the tale. I'll also tell you why I haven't been able to use it yet. It's important and interesting stuff."

"I've got lots of homework," Laura said, realizing the way in would be thanks to a key—something she had expected. "Maybe you can tell me another time?"

"Sure, sure. You got the goods?"

"Yeah." Laura reached into her schoolbag. She placed the bottle of vodka on the counter in front of Ivan, then glanced around the diner—no one was interested in their exchange.

"Excellent." Ivan procured the key—which looked like any other door key—and held it in his open palm. "Pretty nifty, huh? Bet you didn't think I was such a cool cat." He closed his hand, concealing the key. "Oh, I almost forgot. I have a question for you first."

Laura wanted to curse, but she kept her cool. "What is it?"

"Do you know why the town is called Goohill?"

Was this a test? Ivan wasn't seeking the standard answer: the town was named after one of its founders, David Goodhill, but a spelling error had created the current name. He wanted one of the other answers, of which there were many. Locals knew there was no *real* answer, at least not one which they all agreed upon.

"It's called Goohill because there used to be an illegal waste facility on one of the hills outside of town. There was an explosion and green goo ended up coming down the hill. It caused a lot of damage to the environment and even made a few people sick."

Ivan chuckled. "Oh, Laura. You can't believe that one. Why honor such a tragic event?" He handed her the key.

Laura shrugged and placed the key in her bag, while Ivan retrieved a small silver flask from his pants pocket. He filled the flask with his newly acquired vodka, then smiled.

"You tell me the answer then," Laura said. "Why is the place called Goohill?"

Ivan took a swig of vodka from the bottle. "Well, today, I believe it's because an alien appeared to one of the early locals. The visitor tried to communicate, but we weren't advanced enough to decipher their language. All the local could remember from the event was the alien's name. It wasn't any word he knew, so the best he could do was...Goohill."

"And why honor that? That's so dumb."

"It's mysterious. The kind of thing small-town locals love to honor. But hey," Ivan said, getting up from his seat, "ask me again tomorrow. I'm sure I'll have heard a different story for the town's name by then."

Ivan grabbed the bottle of vodka and placed it in his bag. "Well, I'm off. Good luck on your quest. If you discover anything cool, let me know."

Laura nodded.

"And...be careful of ole Edith. She's a real wet rag and would flip her lid if she caught you snooping around."

Ivan greeted a few people before exiting the diner.

Laura remained at the counter, thinking about what she was about to do, dreaming about what she might unearth. A moment of apprehension passed into one of excitement. She knew the library well. If things went her way, this could be not only an easy task, but one filled with answers to many mysteries, and perhaps even some new tales of the town.

She surveyed the diner, and as her gaze trailed back to the counter, she caught sight of a beaten-up navy-blue baseball cap. Ivan had been in such a rush to enjoy the vodka that he'd forgotten his cap.

Laura dropped the cap into her bag and headed for the diner's exit, hoping to catch Ivan outside.

* * *

This wasn't Laura's first time in the library, nor was it her first time trying to gain access to the back rooms. Getting to the green door that led to the narrow hallway with its four rooms was never too hard a task—made even easier today by the fact that the head librarian, Edith, was nowhere in sight. The two younger librarians were usually too caught up in gossiping about the town's latest drama to be an obstacle.

Today had been no different.

After Laura entered the hallway, the four doors stood before her—two on either side of her. The first on her left was a bathroom. The first to her right was an office—probably Edith's. The last two doors were both locked. Which one did the key unlock? A fear that the key led to a cleaning closet gripped her chest. She focused her breathing, allowing the fear to flow through her before dissipating. Excitement replaced the fear; it fluttered in her core.

She marched to the second door on her left.

She got the key out.

At first it was difficult to align the key to the keyhole with the slight shake in her hands, but she persevered. What secrets would she uncover? Would she know the truth to the town's name? What other answers to the town's myriad of mysteries lay hidden in the room?

The door unlocked.

She entered.

A cough startled her as she closed the door leading back to the hallway. It didn't emanate from the room she was in. Maybe it came from the office? Was it Edith? It didn't matter. Laura had come too far. She waited for the sound of approaching footsteps.

None arrived.

She turned back to the room.

The area was much bigger than she had anticipated. Rows of dusty shelves filled with old books and newspapers ate most of the room's space. A large wooden desk to her left caught her attention; an assortment of stationery and tools for repairing damaged books covered most of the desk's surface. To her far right stood stacks of boxes and filing cabinets filled with a cornucopia of peculiar objects, from an old cast-iron pot to a pistol rusted with history.

The room was perfect.

It exceeded her expectations.

Laura started rummaging through the cabinets at the back. A plethora of documents, newspapers, photographs, drawings, and maps greeted her. This was truly a treasure trove; she shook her head, berating herself for not making a stronger concerted effort to explore the library earlier. Moving to some shelves to her left, she came across what appeared to be censuses of the town.

A door slammed, and she jolted, first fearing it was the door to the room she was in, but the sound had been too distant. Maybe the office? Was someone coming here? She ducked low, listening intently.

Footsteps approached, but they didn't stop before the room. Instead, the person continued, heading into the main library area.

"Shit," Laura muttered. There was too much stuff for her to go through in one session. Anyone could enter at any time, and if they did, she would never get in again. She needed to be clever and search a section, then retreat until she could return and attack another area.

Heading to the right, she intended to dig through boxes in the rear of the room. They appeared old—dusty and beaten up. She moved the first one away, only for an antique goblet to fall through the bottom of the box.

It clanged on the floor.

How loud had the noise truly been? To Laura it had sounded like someone banging a drum next to her ear, but she knew that was because she was highly alert, nervous, and excited. Maybe it hadn't been as loud as she'd feared? Maybe no one had heard?

"Is someone here?"

It was Edith.

She was in the hallway.

"Come out now or I will have the police drag you out."

Laura couldn't reveal herself. If she did, she would never be able to enter the library again. What could she do? For all her efforts to be ruined by one clumsy mistake was unacceptable.

Footsteps thundered outside the door. Perspiration built under Laura's arms and on her forehead, while her heart beat in her throat, booming so loud she feared it would be audible to Edith. She expected the door to the room to swing open. It didn't. A door not too far away, however, did creak open. Was it the one for the room next door? It must've been.

Laura needed a plan.

One came to her. It wasn't ideal but had the potential for success. She dug in her schoolbag and retrieved Ivan's baseball cap; she had planned to give it to him at the diner, but he'd been gone by the time she got outside.

"Sorry," she said, placing the cap on one of the shelves.

Below the shelf was a leather satchel.

A combination of desperation and intrigue swirled within Laura. She didn't want to leave with nothing. The satchel had an allure, almost as if it whispered to her, "Open me. Look inside." Laura couldn't resist the urge of discovery that had ascended internally, now towering over her fear. She opened the satchel and peeked inside: a hardcover book lay inside.

She took the book out and held it up, inhaling its dusty aroma. There was strange writing on the front and even weirder symbols. A peculiar static-like feeling erupted over her skin, and she knew she had found something important.

A door opened.

Laura guessed it belonged to the room next to her. It was time to escape, and she held the book under her right arm, doubting it would fit into her schoolbag, especially with all her other stuff inside. She opened the room's door as quietly as she could and stepped out; she was prepared to do whatever it took to get past anyone and escape with her newfound treasure.

Laura didn't see anyone.

She bolted down the hallway, not wasting even a split second to observe her surroundings. She didn't care whether someone caught a glimpse of her or heard her footsteps. All she yearned for now was escape.

Banging the door shut that returned her to the main section of the library, she decided to proceed with more tact and stealth, and she decreased her pace until it resembled a casual walk. Had she been lucky? Had Edith seen her? For some reason, she felt as if she had gotten away clean. The thought of Edith finding Ivan's cap came to the fore, but she slapped it away with haste. She clutched the book closely, tightly, as she headed for the exit of the library, moving between shelves, trying to avoid anyone.

A loud roar, like a wounded animal, erupted from behind her. It sounded like Edith shouting "No!" but the sound was guttural, angry, yet sorrowful.

Laura exited the library without looking back. Once she got beyond its exterior gates, she dashed home.

Her treasure remained safe in her arms.

What secrets did it hold?

THE BRIDGE THAT SHOULD NOT BE

Mercy. Mercy. Mercy.

Bill Simpson had purposefully repeated her name over and over with the rhythmic monitoring of a metronome as he walked away from his vehicle. She no longer went by the name she had when they'd been in school together. What had caused the change? He didn't know and he hadn't pried. She would likely explain it all to him once she was ready. What he did know was that he had fallen for her. She was unlike anyone else in their little town—special, unique, or both? It was hard to describe her in a way that was fitting of her mesmerizing existence. Not everyone felt the way he did about her. In fact, a few people had even warned him not to get too close to her, but they had to be either jealous or dumb.

He had telephoned her earlier, while finishing at work, hoping to meet up, but she'd informed him that she had an errand to run first at the bridge outside of town. That had thrown him initially, but he remembered that she'd developed an almost insatiable hunger for knowledge of the town's history. She probably wanted to document something about the bridge for her files. It had hit him after he'd ended the call. He could help. Who wouldn't want a partner on an excursion?

Walking to the center of the two-lane arched-stone bridge revealed no one. Had she already left? A more worrisome question arose: had Mercy lied to him? He shook his head, trying to incinerate the thought. Voices called his attention and he calmed himself, listening intently, hoping that his trip wasn't in vain.

"You didn't say anything about being naked."

"So what? No one will see us."

The voices came from below. Bill stepped closer to the bridge's railing, feeling confident that he recognized one of the voices while growing sure he knew who the other belonged to as well.

His assumptions had been correct, except he hadn't expected to see Mercy naked from head to toe. She stood in the center of a starlike symbol with a circle around it drawn onto a white sheet with permanent marker. Burning candles sat at various points on the symbol. Next to Mercy stood her good friend Nancy. Nancy was fully clothed, wearing a white jersey with blue jeans, and she crossed her arms as she walked away from the bridge, stumbling over the rock-filled dry riverbed. Bill recalled that water had only stopped flowing a decade or two ago, due to some or other industrial accident.

"Come back," Mercy said.

"No." Nancy shook her head. "Anyone could rock up here. I don't feel like getting into any more trouble with your stuff."

"It needs to be more than just me."

"I'm sorry. You should have mentioned exactly what we would need to do before we got all the way out here."

Nancy increased her speed and marched up the embankment leading back to the bridge. Either she didn't notice Bill or she ignored him as she headed back into town. Bill had considered calling after her, offering her a ride, but that would have meant leaving Mercy—which was unacceptable. When she had disappeared into the distance, he considered his options. Mercy mumbled something from below, almost like singing but not quite. He could announce himself. Would she be happy to see him here? Would she be angry that he saw her naked, or maybe she would think he was a perve? The questions swirled within his mind, reminding him of the time he had gotten nauseous while fishing with his uncle out at sea.

He needed to act.

He couldn't go through life wondering, *What if?*

As he leaned over the railing, he raised his hand and waved. "Hi, Mercy."

She looked up. No signs of anger appeared on her visage, and she remained still with no instinctiveness to cover herself.

"Bill?" she said.

"Yeah."

"Get down here. I need you."

* * *

Dusk was chillier than Bill would've liked. Why couldn't Mercy have chosen summer as the perfect time for her shenanigans? He had already stripped and joined Mercy in the peculiar symbol she had drawn; she had called the symbol "a pentacle." As they had stood together, she taught him some of the phrases he needed to repeat with her. They were Latin phrases according to Mercy, and they had taken him a few minutes to get the hang of. Mercy hadn't grown frustrated with him; she had remained calm, almost too calm, as if she were under the influence of some drug.

How long would they have to keep repeating the phrases? He wasn't sure, and he wanted to ask her but he feared that halting the ritual would lead them to having to perform it from the beginning again. Instead, he wondered what the hell they were doing... What was the ritual for?

He had forgotten to inquire.

He made a mental note to ask her the first opportunity he got.

A warm breeze came out of nowhere, wrapping around his chest before retreating to wherever it had emanated from. Bill glanced around. A tingling sensation briefly infiltrated his eyes, causing him to reach up to rub them, but as he performed the action, the sensation vanished. Tiny blue lights flickered in his peripheral vision, and he turned his neck, attempting to catch a better view. The lights hovered, like cerulean fireflies riding a zephyr. They drifted toward him, then congregated in front of him and Mercy. He was reasonably sure that he wasn't imagining them, but to put his mind at ease, he looked at Mercy.

"Do you see them?"

She nodded while repeating the Latin phrases.

"What the hell is going on?"

"Keep repeating what I taught you."

The roar of an engine and bright lights overhead caused Bill to step back, outside of the pentacle. The blue lights that had floated around them had vanished.

Mercy grabbed his arm. "What are you doing?"

"Look up," Bill said. "Someone has stopped on the bridge."

"No! We need to keep the ritual going. I'm not sure if it's done."

"You haven't done it before?"

"No."

A car door slammed above them. Bill tugged on Mercy's arm. "Let's book it before we're in serious shit."

She didn't answer, but by the way she dropped her shoulders, he sensed that she wouldn't put up a fight.

He didn't want to head under the bridge, fearful movement in the open and right under the newcomer would alert the uninvited stranger to their whereabouts. So, he guided Mercy to a group of bushes to their right, about a third of the way up the embankment. They ducked behind the flora, even though he realized that due to the season it didn't have many leaves to aid them. He hoped that the cover and darkening night would combine and suffice.

Bill peered back at the bridge, trying to identify the man who now leaned over the railing, still oblivious to their ritual below. The man held a bottle—probably beer—and took a swig, then cursed the world around him. He looked familiar. Bill had seen him in town on many occasions, but the man's name evaded him.

"Ivan," Mercy said. "He's causing so much shit lately. Making it hard for me."

"You know him?" Bill asked. "He's behaving like a goof."

"I know him a little."

Ivan grew more animated, and Bill wondered if he was ever going to leave. The man appeared to be on a crusade to spew every curse word created at the world, while drinking his way into an impressive stupor.

"Damn, what's his problem?" Bill whispered.

"He...well, he hasn't been the same since he got caught snooping around the library. A librarian claimed he stole stuff, but the cops couldn't prove it."

"The library? Who wants a bunch of dusty books?"

Mercy scoffed. "Sometimes you can be so stupid. There's a lot more to the library than meets the eye."

Bill didn't believe the library held anything other than boring old books, but the insult from Mercy stung. He didn't like it and didn't want to give her cause to sting him again.

"Yeah, you're right," he said. "If he wasn't charged, why did it affect him so much?"

"One of the librarians, Edith, she caused a lot of problems for him. She protects the library and whatever it holds. Ivan lost his job, and he couldn't get another in town. He would do some freelance work, but even that dried up as Edith's whispers spread around town."

"Damn, okay. I didn't know all that."

A bottle shattered a few feet from them. Bill jolted, but he remained hidden behind the bush. Mercy appeared unperturbed. Glancing back at Ivan, Bill noticed that he was bending over the railing, staring directly at their pentacle.

"I think he sees it," Bill said.

Mercy didn't reply.

"What the fuck is going on down there?" Ivan screamed. "Show yourselves, now!"

Neither Bill nor Mercy did.

Ivan leaned farther over the bridge, gazing into the blackening realm, ignoring the new beer he held.

"Should we run?" Bill asked Mercy.

Before Mercy could respond, Ivan fell forward, over the bridge. A faint scream emanated from him before he crashed onto the hard ground beneath the bridge. The bottle of beer shattered next to him. The moment had been over in a flash. One second Ivan was standing on the bridge having a beer, and the next he was lying inert on the ground.

"Holy shit." Bill stood with his hands held up. "Holy shit."

* * *

The warmth from the ritual earlier had vanished. If anything, the chill in the atmosphere had grown more potent, creating the sensation of an icicle piercing Bill's chest as he surveyed Ivan's fallen body. At first, he had jumped up to help but once he'd neared, he realized there wasn't much he could do. Ivan lay motionless; his body had twisted and contorted in an unnatural state. Blood pooled around his head and torso. Ivan had fallen almost perfectly in the center of the pentacle Mercy had drawn earlier. Unfortunately, only hard rocks under the sheet had awaited his fall.

A hand tugged on Bill's arm.

"We have to go," Mercy said. "If we're spotted here, I won't be able to continue my work."

"Work? What? We need to alert the authorities."

"There's nothing we can do for him. He's dead. It's not our fault. They will think it's a suicide anyway."

"Yeah, but it wasn't. He fell because of the ritual shit."

"He fell because he was drunk."

"It just feels odd leaving him. What about your sheet?"

"Leave it."

"They'll know someone was here."

Mercy didn't reply; she dressed instead. Bill reluctantly did the same while struggling to come out of the daze that had smothered him after seeing Ivan fall. Conflicted, he wished he knew the right course of action. He thought he did, but Mercy's words were powerful, and they revealed cracks in values he had once considered concrete.

Mercy picked up the backpack she had brought along. "There are secrets to this town, Bill. Stuff they don't like people knowing. I've been investigating. I can show and tell you things that would blow your mind. But the question is, can I trust you?"

"Of course you can. I'm no square."

He was intrigued. That he couldn't deny. He had heard whispers and rumors of the town's past, and even its current undertakings. Goohill was a peculiar place, and it wasn't only new visitors who felt that way.

Mercy held his hand. "Let's go. I've got so much to show you."

Ivan's vehicle's floodlights continued to shine in the night. It wouldn't be long before someone came along. They would spot him; they would report the accident. Bill and Mercy hadn't done anything wrong, technically, so why create unnecessary drama for themselves? Maybe Mercy was right after all?

She kissed him on the cheek. "Thank you for coming here tonight and for helping me. I've always been able to count on you."

He looked at her. "And you will always be able to."

"Would you jump off a bridge for me?"

Bill chuckled. Even in their current situation, he couldn't deny that Mercy's dark sense of humor never failed to make things feel a little better. "Yeah, of course I would."

THE TOWN THAT FEARED DUSK

A GIFT FROM THE BRIDGE

Maya Vogel sipped her glass of merlot, imagining she could cast a spell that would bring her boyfriend, Clayton, to her at once. Reality was cruel; she knew nothing that could make him magically appear, at least not yet, and she gulped the rest of her wine down instead.

Gazing at one of the bookshelves, she considered giving the latest book she had bought on witchcraft a read. Her mind wandered, however, and feelings of uncertainty regarding the future draped over her thoughts, making them heavier than the gray clouds that had filled the sky during the afternoon.

She loved Clayton. He loved her, even if he sometimes didn't express that in the clearest and warmest ways. Her job as a personal assistant was going well, but Clayton had a dead-end job working as a waiter at a local restaurant.

He could do so much better.

If only she could think of a way to motivate him.

Maybe a spell for positivity? That was a great idea, and she stood to search the drawers near her for some candles.

Keys rattled outside the front door, stopping her.

The keys clanged on the ground.

"Shit," Clayton said from outside.

Maya walked to the door and unlocked it for him; he picked up the keys and entered with a cheesy grin.

"You're late." She gave him a kiss on the cheek. "You said you'd be home before it got dark."

"Yeah. I went a few extra places."

Maya led him to the living room.

She knew he'd gone to see his aunt, who worked at a diner in a nearby town, but she had no idea what "extra places" meant. He'd wanted Maya to go with him on his trip, but Clayton had only recently gotten to know his aunt again after years of not having any kind of relationship with her. After his parents passed away, she was almost the only family he had left. Maya wanted them to catch up without her as a third wheel, at least for now, or so she told herself.

Another reason existed for her not going: the town his aunt stayed in. The people were unfriendly, the weather was perpetually inclement, and the place had a vibe that made her anxious. She had once told a friend that the town gave her the heebie-jeebies. She stood by that statement.

As she took a seat on the sofa, she noticed a spot of dirt on Clayton's jacket. "Where all did you go?"

"To my aunt first," Clayton said. "Had lunch at the diner, was great. Oh, she got upset on the phone when someone tried asking her questions about a bridge on the other side of her town. She even slammed the phone. Can you believe that?"

"Let me guess: you went to the bridge."

"Well, she didn't want to talk about the bridge at first, got all weird. But when the diner was empty after lunch, I kept on and she told me a little bit about it. You'd love it. It's meant to be haunted or something. I can't remember everything she said—well, other than I should avoid it, especially during the evening."

"A haunted bridge? That could be bad energy, like if someone cursed the place, or a horrific event stained it in negative energy. That's if it is truly haunted," Maya said. Sure, the town was a bit odd, but she didn't fall for every haunting story. She believed some places were haunted, but they were much rarer than people would have you believe.

"I thought you're into the weird stuff?"

Maya shook her head. "You know better than that."

"I'm kidding. I'm kidding. You're a good witch. I know."

Maya sighed. Three years together, and Clayton still didn't understand her interest in magick and witchcraft. She focused on doing good, strengthening positive energy, and healing. "I hope you didn't go to the bridge."

"Well." Clayton smirked and pulled down on his shirt, revealing a black string around his neck. He lifted out a piece of stone attached to the cord. "I actually made this for you. It was a part of the bridge."

Maya groaned. "You never listen."

"I do. Check this thing out. There's even a symbol drawn on it. It sure looks a lot like the ones in your books."

Maya got up and inspected the stone. "It looks like half a symbol... Hmm... And someone drew over it with another. I can't make out what it is. You only got a piece—"

"Damn. Do you know how hard it was to get? First I had to make it down below the bridge, which was a pain in the ass. Then I had to take a rock and toss it against the bridge until I found a weak spot. It took a few throws until this bad boy fell. I thought it was so cool when I saw it had drawings on it."

"Is that how you got dirty?"

"That and the cop."

"A cop?"

"Yeah, but don't worry," Clayton said, giving the thumbs-up. "It was dusk when he stopped his car nearby, and I was done with the bridge, so I'm pretty sure he never saw me."

Maya forced a smile, even though agitation pricked her skin all over, like tiny bugs feasting on her flesh. How many times had she told Clayton not to get involved in things he didn't understand?

Clayton took the necklace off and handed it to her. "Here you go."

"Thanks, Clayton," she said, taking it. "Now, I'm going to the bathroom to get ready for dinner. You can pour yourself a glass of wine. I've already opened a bottle."

* * *

The cool water soothed Maya, and she splashed another handful on her face, then massaged her forehead with the tips of her fingers. She closed the tap, looking at the peculiar necklace sitting on the bathroom counter. What harm could it do to wear it for a few minutes? She didn't want to hurt Clayton's feelings. Maybe she should do a cleansing spell first? To be safe.

She searched the drawer to her left, as she usually kept sage there, but found none.

A loud *bang* came from the living room.

"Clayton, what are you up to?" Maya asked.

Thinking back, she realized he had been acting a little odd since returning home. He'd appeared timid, and a little goofier than usual. What could it be? Had he enjoyed a drink or two on his trip? She hadn't smelled alcohol on him. Maybe he wanted to surprise her with something more than the handmade gift? He was bad at keeping surprises.

A lighter flicked from beyond the bathroom door.

"Clayton, please don't burn the place down."

"Don't worry. I won't," Clayton replied.

More flicks of the lighter followed. Was Clayton trying to create a romantic atmosphere? That would explain the gift and his quirky behavior. The idea settled, and she smiled at his cute attempt to show her love. Would he throw rose petals on the floor next? Put on some love ballads? She debated giving him more time, but when she heard another *bang*, louder than the first, she decided his time to prepare was up.

The necklace caught her eye.

She put it around her neck, then glanced at herself in the bathroom mirror before exiting, eager to see Clayton's idea of a romantic evening.

* * *

Clayton sat naked on the living room floor, surrounded by lit candles. He had drawn a pentagram in black on the wooden floor around himself.

"Clayton, what are you doing?" Maya asked, stepping into the living room. The scene wasn't romantic at all. Was this another one of his silly jokes? She hoped the pen he had used wasn't permanent. That wouldn't be funny.

"It's a ritual, babe. This evening, we will prove our love for each other."

"What are you talking about? Signs like that aren't jokes. Put some clothes on and clean up this mess." She wanted to storm out but resisted. "This isn't funny."

Clayton didn't appear perturbed by her reaction, and he rummaged in a brown bag sitting alongside him. He pulled out a dagger. "I got this today too."

"Clayton, you're freaking me out. Stop this nonsense, now."

He got to his knees. "An old woman at the bridge wanted me to do something for her, but I told her I couldn't as I had to get back to you. She said this is how you and I can prove our love for each other. This is how we will be together, forever."

"What old woman?"

Clayton's eyes possessed a glossy look, one that he had never exhibited before. Was he under...a spell? He started to mumble words that sounded Latin, but they weren't ones Maya could recall encountering in her studies.

A heat rose in Maya's chest, emanating from the stone. The warmth worsened every time Clayton repeated his new learned phrase. "Clayton, what are you doing? Please stop."

He repeated the phrase once more, then said, "I love you, Maya. We will be together for eternity now." He lowered the dagger so that the blade pierced his gut.

Blood exited the wound, then flowed down his genitals and legs. He winced but plunged the weapon deeper.

Maya needed to escape, but a numbness had beset her as disorientation turned her into its marionette. The heat in her chest had grown stronger and had spread throughout her body. Its intensity exploded, and it rivaled the heat of the sun.

She battled herself, demanding that her right arm reach up and rip the cursed necklace from her being, but the limb refused her command.

Instead, her body moved forward, toward Clayton.

It wasn't the direction she wanted to go.

Clayton had dropped forward. Blood ran out the corners of his mouth, covered his lower half, and pooled across the floor.

The sensation of fire now filled every atom of Maya's being, and whispers echoed behind the smoke clouding her mind. The whispers combined into one strong voice, and it dawned on her how much she loved

Clayton. It was an inferno of emotion nothing could extinguish. He was right. They had to prove their love for each other. They would be together forever.

She pulled the dagger out of Clayton's abdomen. "Wait, my love. I want to journey with you to our paradise."

She raised the blade and cut her throat.

THE HOUSE THAT REMAINED

He hadn't greeted anyone, opting to avoid eye contact with everyone and everything. Not acknowledging anybody's existence meant being efficient. So, where had he gone wrong? It was his first misstep in a long, long time. Complacency was dangerous. He cursed under his breath as he marched home, relegating the grocery store to the past. Looking down, he scanned over the shopping list in his hand. He had procured all the items in what he felt to be a competent excursion. Where had he gone wrong? The question evolved into a refrain, but no answer arrived to bring him any sense of comfort.

He crossed the road, barely glancing for traffic.

His house was the only place that felt safe.

The house had remained when all other friends and family had said their goodbyes, stopped visiting, and then ceased calling. He hadn't been able to move on like everyone else. Sure, he had considered leaving Goohill. Family members and a few friends had mentioned or offered opportunities near to them. None of the job offers or prospects of work had enticed him enough to pack up and relocate. Was he punishing himself? He could have done more; he should've done more.

Thoughts of Letitia entered his mind's eye, and the ephemeral images offered a faint sense of hope, warmth even, but he knew better. There was only coldness and nothingness residing in the nightmare that was the past.

He upped his pace, unconcerned how he might come across.

He yearned for his home.

* * *

It was when he passed the hardware store that he sensed her company—not Letitia's, but rather she who he didn't want to name. Her presence started as a coldness draping over his hands, then an unnerving sensation of someone or something watching him. He glanced behind: no visible figure trailed him—yet. Where could she be? She had grown more powerful and the rules that'd once applied to her unnatural existence seemed to be waning, unlike for the others, who appeared to have their movements confined to one location during dusk. Why did she have to be different? Why did she have to target him? There were so many other people in town.

He didn't want to do her bidding. She was responsible for what had happened to Letitia, and though he had no evidence, a gut feeling consolidated and assured him he was correct.

As he rounded the chemist, heading up a narrow alley, shadows shifted extraordinarily. She was here. He increased his pace, and he considered his options. The desire to drop his groceries and run came to the fore of his mind. Would that work? Could one outrun the shadows? The questions were futile, as he already knew the answers. When she had first come for him, he'd tried to elude her, but she could simply appear where he least expected it. He needed to outsmart her. That approach had worked on the rare occasion, making it the best option.

A plan presented itself: he required an unexpected route home, even if it took him longer. That might throw her off. Through the park? If there were people, she might resist confronting him.

He altered his direction.

* * *

The park appeared larger than expected, as if its grassy plain continuously expanded, stretching beyond a distance he could run without needing a break. Nonsense, of course, but fear has a unique way of playing tricks on the mind. He breathed in deep, making sure he kept a steady pace, while mumbling choice curse words as he realized there was no one in the park but him. Where were the kids playing baseball or the couples walking their dogs when you needed them?

As he attempted to cross the road after the park, a white car stopped in front of him. The window rolled down. It wasn't her, which brought some relief, as even a stranger was more comforting than the chill of her attendance.

"Hey," a man with dark-rimmed glasses said. "I'm sorry to bug you. I was wondering if you could help me with something."

"With what?"

The man reached out with his hand. "I'm Jimmy Rydell."

"Dave Daytona," Dave said, reluctantly shaking the man's hand. He glanced around, thankful that shadows didn't creep toward him.

"Nice to meet you, Dave. You a local?"

Dave nodded. "You need directions?"

"Not exactly. I've got some questions about a bridge outside your lovely town. I can't stay long, just passing through. I intend on coming back some time to dig a little deeper. I'm thinking of taking a quick peep at the place before I leave."

"I'm sorry. I'm busy at the moment."

"Too busy for a few questions?"

"I'm afraid so."

Dave paced away from the vehicle as fast as his feet would carry him. He didn't care if he acted a fool, as all that mattered now was the safety of home. The outsider's questions were an ominous sign. The callous mention of the bridge alerted the shadows the same way blood in the water triggered sharks. The outsider's car started up in his wake and the man honked, but Dave didn't lose a step.

If she was watching, she would be angry, very, very, angry.

On one occasion when she had caught him, she'd offered him an ultimatum after he refused to do her bidding: he was to direct any newcomers, especially those with an interest in the bridge—and there were a few of those over the years—to her home. He had agreed, hoping it would get her off his back, and it had for a while, even though he never did direct anyone anywhere. Someday, he knew, he would have to cave to her demand and send some poor soul to her wicked abode.

Today was not that day.

Today he wouldn't accept defeat.

Sensing her presence again, he ducked into the yard of one of the homes to his right. He dashed round the back of the house, thankful for the unlocked side-gate. In the backyard, he headed straight for the wooden fence at its rear. His adrenaline ran strong, and he was able to scale and jump over the fence on the first effort.

He crossed the next road, now able to see his house in the distance.

A mellifluous voice called out to him.

Was it time to run?

Shadows stretched over the road to his right, and they formed sharp spikes, almost clawlike, as they reached for him. She was hunting him. He held his hands to his ears, attempting to block out her call, but it was difficult with the grocery bag. What to do? He wouldn't be able to fool her again so quickly. Her call grew more potent, almost evolving into a cry, yearning for him. The urge to turn and surrender coursed through his nervous system. His own body was turning against him as the constant battle with her over the years wore him down. What to do?

"Fuck it," he said, dropping his groceries.

He sprinted for his home.

* * *

The houses to his side appeared to blur, but he knew it wasn't from his speed—which had slowed with age—or their similar designs, but instead due to fear. The fear had caused his vision to narrow to an almost tunnel-like view of his house. As the initial burst of adrenaline wore off, it didn't take long for his troublesome left knee to throb with pain, and if that wasn't enough, a burning sensation had erupted in the middle of his chest. His exhales were loud. How out of shape had he let himself become? He made a mental note that he needed to do more cardiovascular exercise if he escaped her today. He needed to be in better shape for moments such as these. The thoughts helped him focus, and he ignored his audible breathing and the sound of his shoes hitting the road.

He listened for her.

This brought slight relief, as her call had disappeared. Maybe she was too far back? Maybe another target had taken her interest? Maybe her strength had waned for the day? His arrival home helped ease the burning in his chest. His knee still hurt as he darted into his yard, following the cracked stone path, and scurried up the four steps to his front door. He had instinctively grabbed the key from his pocket when entering his yard, so he wouldn't waste time fumbling for it once at the door.

He stumbled in, then smashed the door closed behind him, not daring to peek at the outside world he had left behind. After locking the door, he gave himself a moment to catch his breath, then moved through the house, making sure all the windows were closed and all the curtains drawn.

He sat in his living room, wiping away the sweat that had formed on his brow. Bracing himself, he expected to hear her screams, threatening and attacking him, but all was still in the house that remained.

THE TOWN THAT FEARED DUSK

SHOWDOWN AT THE LIBRARY

The shift had been seismic. The previous day, Ashley Tanner had berated her life choices that'd led her to having to work at the town's diner at twenty-four, causing her to question her will to even exist. Today, she had awoken with a path and a purpose. The new thoughts swirled internally, troubling her at first, but as the day progressed, the ideas gained clarity and traction in her mind. Who would've guessed that going to the bridge on the outside of town the previous night would have brought her some hope? She had initially gone there to wallow in her misery. It was a depressing place after all, considering there had been suicides there, but no, she never intended to jump off the bridge, as some had done in the past. She simply wanted to peer over the bridge and wonder what it would be like to be somewhere else. What would it be like to find the perfect place?

"Okay, you can go. You're free. I still need to sort out some admin stuff before I leave," Tammy Washburn, the elder server, said from behind the counter.

"Thanks, Tams." Ashley marched straight for the exit, not glancing back, and grabbed her jersey off one of the tables near the door.

Outside, she sighed.

She wasn't free yet.

She slowed her pace, ambling toward a dusty red pickup in the parking lot. The pickup belonged to Peyton Garcia, the diner's cook and her ride home, except tonight she had another destination in mind. Resting her elbow on the rear of the vehicle, she turned back to the diner, hoping Tammy wouldn't keep Peyton too long. She had things to do and places to be.

Seconds passed.

Thoughts circulated.

"Finally." She raised her arms in a mini celebration as Peyton approached from the bright lights of the diner. "I was getting worried Tammy was gonna keep you all night."

"I was like a minute or two after you," Peyton said, walking to the driver's side of his vehicle. "Well, you mentioned you weren't heading straight home. Where did you need a lift to?"

* * *

"We're here," Peyton said, tapping his fingers on the steering wheel. "Definitely not where I thought I'd drop you off."

Ashley shrugged. There was far more activity outside of the police station than she had expected. Two police officers stood like sentries in front, talking to an old man wearing a long brown coat. To their left, a middle-aged couple debated over some piece of paper the woman held. A black cat sauntered past the police station, seemingly oblivious to the humans around it.

Ashley glanced down, nodding when she laid eyes on the small red sports bag she had brought with. It contained the goods she would require for the night. The items were rudimentary as she didn't want to attract any unnecessary attention. This approach had also led to her needing to purchase the supplies at several spots around town during her lunch break. The bag helped calm her nerves. The bag meant she was one step closer to changing the direction of her life.

"What are we doing here, anyway?" Peyton asked. "You lose something? Something get stolen? I heard those Rowley brothers have been loitering around again. They're always up to no good."

Ashley shook her head.

"Well, what is it?"

"I can't tell you. You wouldn't understand."

Peyton shrugged. "What? You and I have shared so much... Have I ever not understood anything?"

"This is different."

Peyton huffed and stared out the driver's-side window. Ashley didn't want to waste the energy required to pacify him. Peyton's poor mood would devolve further into sulking, and then there would be much moaning and groaning. Would he understand? She considered the question. He had surprised her in the past, and having him on her side would be greatly beneficial, as time was a key factor in her mission. Once she executed the first move, others would be on the defensive, and some might even go on the offensive. If she erred or took too long on the next objectives, things would only continue to increase in difficulty. Would he understand? They had often spoken of similar dreams and desires. Still, it was unlikely that he would assist her even if he did agree with her mission, but then again, she didn't need an assistant—she needed a ride.

Ashley turned to Peyton. "I'll tell you what I'm doing when we get to the next stop."

"You're not getting out here?"

"No. It's too...busy."

"Ah, okay." Peyton started the engine. "Where to next, then?"

* * *

The old Gothic-style church, with its spires atop its stone towers piercing the night sky, stood tall, watching over the town. Its stained-glass windows mesmerized as light posts, erected in its yard, greeted them. Someone, however, had locked the large black steel gates that surrounded the church. That couldn't be, could it? The gates were almost always open.

"Shit," Ashley said, slapping her leg.

"What now?" Peyton asked. "I didn't take you for the super religious type. What are we doing here? You said you'd tell me."

She had, hadn't she? How could she phrase her newfound purpose so that Peyton would recognize she had the best intentions for Goohill? Did it matter if he understood? She had grown cold at the prospect of revealing all to him. A voice in her mind gave her clarity: it didn't matter whether he understood or not, as all that mattered was that she accomplished her goals. He would gain lucidity and thank her once her vision came to fruition—and so would many others. What if he spoke and caused her trouble? Well, then he would have to pay the price.

"Tell me," Peyton said.

"Are you sure you want to know? If I tell you, there can be no going back."

"Sheesh, you make it sound all serious." Peyton shut off the engine. "We've shared many secrets. I've never let you down."

"I know, but these are matters on another level. You can't tell a soul. Do you agree to that?"

"Sure."

"I'm not joking around, Peyton."

"I'm not either. I won't tell a soul."

"Fine." Ashley inhaled deep then exhaled slowly. "I've always thought about leaving Goohill. You know that?"

Peyton nodded. "Yeah, me too."

"The place isn't right. It's going backward, and I need more. Everyone here needs more. I've often contemplated where and when I would go once I was able to make the move, but then, I had an idea. What if I don't leave? What if I can help Goohill achieve its true potential?"

"How?"

"Well, I realized the unholy trinity are holding the town back."

"The what?"

"The unholy trinity. That's the church, the police station, and the library, including those in charge of them. These three institutions conspire to keep dragging Goohill back into the past, preventing regeneration or new creation. If they were damaged, or even better, destroyed…well, then new opportunities would arise."

A puzzled expression had replaced Peyton's usual friendly countenance. "That makes no—"

"The priest, the police chief, and the head librarian all sit on the town's council. They are heavily invested in what can or can't happen here. If they lose their grip on power, even for a moment, it will allow others in."

"Firstly, what you're considering are serious crimes, as in jail. Secondly, I'm sure they are all insured. They would just rebuild."

"Yes, but there would be a gap for other people in town to make plays to improve it while the unholy trinity remained focused on their rebuilds and other things. They would all take hits, weakening them. Don't you understand?"

"Um, what? And how would you know what other people in town want to do? Most talk at the diner is just that: talk. I've told you before. I can also say a lot of shit and brag about a lot of amazing plans I have. To commit crimes—"

"I knew you wouldn't understand."

Peyton didn't respond, and an uncomfortable silence invaded the small space of the vehicle. Why had she hoped for his understanding? Why had she thought he would be any different? People were so disappointing. Why couldn't they see the bigger picture? Why did they all want to sit around and wait until someone had done everything for them? One day, Peyton would thank her for her actions.

"I can't go here now with the locked gates. I'm not prepared. I'll have to alter my plans. Can you take me to another location?"

"I'll drop you off somewhere, but I am not getting more involved. I'm telling you all that's going to happen is you will end up in jail. You're not thinking straight."

It was disappointing...so, so disappointing. What had happened to Peyton? She considered asking him that exact question but didn't, as the energy wasted on him was already beyond what was acceptable. There were more important things to do, much more important things.

"Can I take you home?" Peyton asked, staring ahead.

"No. You can take me to the library."

"The what?"

"The library."

Peyton shook his head as he started up the vehicle. "Well, here we go again, I guess."

* * *

Ashley strolled down the stone path, attempting to not look out of place, which was difficult as few entered the library grounds this late at night. Garden lights flanked her alongside the path, illuminating her way. The library appeared deserted, but the gates were open. A brief smile formed on her face. When Peyton had dropped her off, she'd warned him again about speaking of her mission. He had come across distant, cold. Unease had squirmed within her, but there was no going back now.

The bag she had brought swung at her side as she increased her pace. Soon, she would implement the first stage of her plan and things would feel better as a new direction heralded a new world. She marched up a set of green-painted concrete stairs, which led her straight for the library's main entrance. Her first action was to start a fire near the library's large wooden front doors. If anyone was inside, which she doubted, they would have enough opportunity to escape via the rear of the building.

A mural of various historic figures on her left called attention, and she couldn't help but try and guess some of them: a Roman soldier, an astronaut, a caveman, and a detective were the first figures that caught her eye.

"Who's there?" a female voice shouted from within the library.

Ashley ceased her forward momentum and stepped back. One of the library's front doors stood ajar. A light popped on above the doors, illuminating her. She had been lost in her own thoughts, not realizing that the library was more awake than it'd first appeared. Footsteps approached.

"Oh, fuck." She turned and ran.

A *bang* boomed behind her. Maybe one of the doors had slammed? She didn't dare glance back, fearful of locking eyes with her pursuer. As she hurtled down the concrete steps, she heard the patter of feet—they were getting closer and moving faster. She had hoped the person would leave her be once she'd retreated, but they had decided to run after her instead.

"Ashley Tanner! Is that you?"

Ashley recognized the voice. It was Edith, the head librarian—but that couldn't be as she was old, ancient even. People in town had often joked that either Edith was a vampire or she drank the blood of children, as it didn't appear she would ever die and give up her position at the library. There was no way she would be able to keep up with Ashley.

"Ashley, stop now and explain yourself."

Ashley upped her pace, unsure of how Edith was able to run and speak at the same time. A tightness had taken hold of Ashley's chest, but she pressed through the discomfort and headed into the road.

"Never thought you would be pulled over to their side. I will stop you just as I've stopped them before."

Ashley couldn't resist, and she glanced back. The woman's face flared with anger, and it seemed as if she was catching Ashley. It couldn't be. Ashley darted across a four-way, not bothering to look in any direction but straight, praying for an escape. A car appeared out of the shadows, barely missing her as the downpour of streetlights illuminated the near miss.

Edith wasn't so lucky.

A *thud* echoed in the night air as the vehicle met flesh and bone.

Ashley stopped and turned around. She looked to the vehicle that had struck Edith, immediately recognizing it as well as the driver who climbed out.

"Oh, fuck," Peyton said, hobbling toward Edith. "What have I done? She just fucking came out of nowhere."

Ashley, even in her shocked state, knew that wasn't true. Peyton had barely missed her and would have had a moment or two to brake had he been watching the four-way and driving within the speed limit. She chose not to correct him.

"Are you okay?" she asked him. A peculiar warmth draped over her body as she looked back to Edith. The shock of moments ago waned fast and something new replaced it. A feeling akin to hope surfaced within. That couldn't be right, could it? She allowed the new sensation to settle; it was welcome.

"I'm fucked." Peyton stopped right before Edith.

Ashley strode to them, then bent down and checked Edith for a pulse. There was none, and Edith had also suffered multiple fractures to her lower limbs. Ashley was not a doctor, but she knew legs weren't meant to be able to form such abnormal positions. Blood pooled around Edith's body. The jokes and rumors about her defying death would cease this week.

"Is she okay?" Peyton asked. "I'll phone an ambulance."

"She's dead."

"Oh fuck, fuck, fuck." Peyton dropped to his knees. "I'm going to spend the rest of my life in fucking jail. I-

I didn't like how I left. I was just coming to see if you were okay."

Ashley scanned her surroundings. Fortunately, it appeared as if the accident hadn't yet awoken the neighborhood.

"I'm so fucked." Peyton wiped a tear that ran down his cheek.

"Oh, Peyton, can you relax?"

"Relax? How?"

"I'll cover for you. I'll tell the authorities I was with you in the car. She came out of nowhere, walking straight into the road. She's old. People will buy it, and you won't have to spend the rest of your life in jail. You just gotta do one thing for me."

"What's that?"

"Help me with my mission."

"Now?"

"No, not now. This will have to die down first. Plus, with her out of the way, I'm sure the other places will be easier."

Peyton didn't respond. Instead, he dropped his gaze. Ashley had caught a glimpse of his visage before he'd opted to stare at the road. He had already conceded to her will and would aid her when required.

She smiled. "Don't worry, everything is going to work out just fine," she said as she started jogging up the road.

"Where are you going?" Peyton asked.

"I've gotta ditch my bag in a bush somewhere, then I'll come back, and we'll report the accident after making sure our story of events matches."

"Oh, yeah, sure, okay."

It had dawned on Ashley that phase one of her plan had gone better than she could've dreamed. Never mind burning down the library, she had cut the head off one of the snakes that infested the town.

Goohill was one step closer to being reborn.

THE TOWN THAT FEARED DUSK

Every journalist has one chance at a story that can change their life forever. That was what Sylvia Bernstein's mentor, Jimmy Rydell, had always told her about the profession. He had been a colleague at the tabloid she worked at until he ended his time in our realm at the age of forty-seven. His desired promotion to editor never came. There was no Pulitzer prize. In fact, there were no awards, unless you count the "Best Daydreamer in the World" mug he had received as a gift from their boss. He never got that one story, the one to direct his life to the path of fame and glory he had envisioned. Instead, he gave himself the consolation prize of a bullet to the brain.

Sylvia had never expected Jimmy to take his own life, as he wasn't the type, but wasn't that what a lot of people say when it happens? Only twenty-eight, she didn't want to end up on the same road as him. A few days after his funeral, she scanned through all the D-list rumors, tips, and stories that gathered figurative dust in the archives of the tabloid's computer system. She needed to find something different from her usual fluff pieces on local celebrities.

A file eventually caught her eye: "Suicide Bridge." Jimmy had opened it a few days before his death, along with adding some notes on a recently created document. Typed in bold on the top of the first page was the line "Must investigate further." Sylvia guessed he never got around to any deeper investigation, though the small town mentioned did ring a bell, albeit faintly. Maybe he had mentioned it to her? She read the notes and other documents; she looked through the photographs.

Her interest grew.

A journey to the bridge took over her schedule.

* * *

It had been a long drive, and Sylvia was thankful for the red-cushioned seats in the diner. She stirred her coffee, looking at the only other customer. The man with thinning gray hair, wearing a denim jacket that had seen many washing cycles, sat at the counter. He tapped his dusty right boot along to the blues music in the background. There were two staff members. One was a female server who looked older than the faded '80s and '90s posters that filled the pastel-yellow walls. Her curly blonde hair bounced up and down as she nodded while reading something on her phone. A burly cook, sporting a near-survivalist beard, whistled out of tune whenever he walked behind the counter. The smells of freshly made coffee and burned onions hung in the air.

Looking at the time on her wristwatch, Sylvia expected more of a rush at dinnertime. Didn't locals like to meet up after work? She reached into the right pocket of her pale pink jacket and placed her notebook on the table, then turned to the first page. There had been thirty-six suicide cases in just under ten years. It was ridiculous that no one had investigated the deaths further, or that she'd never heard of them via other reporters or the news. Was she missing something?

Suicide Bridge, as it had been dubbed, was located right outside of the town. It connected the locals to the world in the east. The deaths caused no real uproar for the local authorities, or so it seemed, as each case fit the suicide bill perfectly and closed as such. Still, Sylvia guessed the locals didn't like to talk about the bridge. She had mentioned it to two men staffing the gas station before town on the west. Their awkward silence would likely become the norm. Tapping her fingers on the cream-colored tabletop, she studied the times of the deaths, noticing a connection.

"Dusk," she whispered.

She looked toward the man seated at the counter and then the server, but neither showed any interest in her. It was as she feared: her questions would be of no use here. Sylvia glanced at her watch, then turned to look outside, estimating she had about thirty minutes until the sun set.

She picked up her car keys.

* * *

The bridge disappointed. Sylvia had left her car running, figuring she would have a look, take some photos, and be off with some inspiration to begin her article. Except there was nothing spectacular about the arched-stone bridge. Simple, weather-beaten, but sturdy railings lined either side of its two-lane road. She had read that the river that once flowed beneath it dried up nearly half a century ago. All she saw below was the dry riverbed filled with rocks, low-growing bushes, and trash.

Standing against the railing, she didn't doubt jumping off the bridge would be effective. The ground looked hard enough to give solid concrete a challenge, and the drop was at least sixty feet. Added to this were the rocks, some sharp, others jagged.

With the last rays of sunlight leaving the road, Sylvia decided to fetch her camera from the car. Still unable to generate any excitement about the bridge, she was surprised at how quiet the area was. Not a single vehicle had passed her since stopping. She wrote it off as small-town mentality, guessing everyone was having dinner and watching their favorite soaps or series or the evening news.

Before she could open her car door, a small blue lightning bolt danced between two bars of the bridge's railing. Taking a few steps closer, Sylvia noticed the same occurrence happening at other points on the bridge. She attributed this phenomenon to a building storm because she had heard these kinds of occurrences could happen.

The sky above was clear.

That was odd.

The little blue lightning bolts vanished, but Sylvia looked around to be sure. Dusk now held her world firmly in its grip. She turned and walked back to the other side of the bridge, hearing an echoey humming sound, like bees trapped in a tin. She reached for the railing but flinched. Static electricity tickled her hands. Sylvia shook them, hoping to get rid of the numbness that lingered.

She stepped back to the railing, careful not to touch it, and peered over.

Something slapped her across the face, but the touch wasn't warm. It felt like ice and caused her to whip her head back to avoid another blow. Her movement was just in time as a near-transparent hand shot down past her face. She looked for it, discovering a strange powder-blue cloud forming below the bridge. Her heart thundered in her chest when the outlines of faces appeared within. She focused. This only cemented her concern as dull eyes and open mouths greeted her. The hand returned in her peripheral vision.

She didn't move fast enough, and it gripped the back of her jacket.

She wriggled like someone possessed, toppling forward onto the bridge. Turning onto her back, she looked up.

It was no longer a hand; it wasn't the image of an apparition she had seen in films, but it could be nothing other than a ghost. It had almost no personal features, and the powder-blue particles that made the earlier cloud constructed its being too. The shape of a body was evident, except it was elongated and its limbs were thin. The hands weren't visible, nor were there any feet.

A pair of marble-white eyes blinked as two arms reached for her. Hands formed. The fingers grew longer, creeping toward her. Sylvia looked to the sides of the abomination; more ghosts had joined the first, and all were coming at her. Some were shorter than the first, but they all shared the same elongated bodies and blurry features. She sprang to her feet, turned, and dashed to her car.

She jumped in and locked the doors.

Her hands trembled as she held the steering wheel, but she managed to pull away, opting not to look back until off the bridge.

The ghosts were gone.

"What the fuck?" Sylvia asked the empty car.

* * *

Sylvia had typed in the address of her next stop after arriving at the bridge, yet when she looked at her location on the GPS, she was driving away from the structure but remained in town. A strange feeling had fallen over her after escaping the bridge, as if she was running on autopilot and guided by something or someone else. It was nonsense, of course; she gripped the steering wheel hard, breathed in deep, and turned around. She followed the GPS's directions again, glancing at her notes to remind herself of the person's name who she intended to visit.

Arriving outside the home of Dave Daytona, Sylvia looked over some of the questions she had prepared, trying to calm her frayed nerves by focusing on the task at hand. Dave's daughter, Letitia, had been one of the thirty-six cases of suicide during the last ten years. Sylvia's interest in the bridge returned fully engaged as the initial potent fear she experienced at the location dissipated. She considered whether it was all some elaborate hoax. Professionals could have faked the imagery, but why bring attention to an area steeped in such a dark history? The callous, frigid touch, however, couldn't be faked. The memory of the icy hand against her skin surfaced.

Sylvia clenched her teeth as the shudder journeyed throughout her body.

She wanted answers.

Finding some level of equilibrium, she climbed out of her car and walked up the cracked stone path that led to the front door. She knocked but got no response. There was an orange glow in one of the windows. Frustrated, she knocked harder, and again, no response came. Sylvia had no other option but to try the door handle.

"Hello," Sylvia said, pushing the unlocked door open. "Is anyone home?"

"Who's there?" a soft male voice asked.

"It's Sylvia Bernstein. I'm a reporter. Is that you, Mister Daytona? I knocked, but no one answered."

"Yes, I heard you, and call me Dave. Now lock the front door, you fool. I didn't lock it in time this evening."

Sylvia did as instructed.

A door to her left unlocked and slowly opened—enough for her to see two wide eyes on a round pale face staring back.

"What do you want?" Dave asked.

"I'm sorry to just walk in, but like I said, I'm a reporter. I'm here investigating the story about the bridge. So far no one wants to talk to me." Sylvia tried to smile. She had decided not to mention her episode at the bridge until she got some answers.

"Of course they won't. Everyone is too scared."

"I'm sorry about what happened to your daughter. It—"

"It wasn't a suicide."

"Well, that's why I'm here." Sylvia motioned to one of the chairs in the living room. "Mind if I have a seat?"

"You can, but I'm not coming out. Not until night, proper night."

Sylvia nodded, deciding to remain standing. A younger version of herself would've found it perplexing how these people could operate happily in the night and feared the ephemeral dusk, but now she knew better. "So, they don't stay out at night?"

Dave opened the door a little wider. His hair was uncombed, and he wore long gray pajamas and navy-blue slippers. "No," he said, shaking his head. "No, they don't. You've seen them? You have, haven't you? Did you see my Letitia?"

"No, um, I don't think so. I did see some of them, but it was quick."

"You're lucky you got away. Most don't, if they get too close. If they do escape, they certainly don't talk about it. I've heard some people go near the bridge trying to get a view of loved ones who've fallen prey to it. Some people only hang around the area, like they're drawn to the place. I can't. I just ca—"

The bedroom door closed.

"Wait," Sylvia said, wondering how long it had been since Dave last left his house.

"Hang on," Dave replied from behind the door. "I'm writing something down for you."

"Okay."

Dave opened the door wide enough to stick his arm out, and he tossed a crumpled-up piece of paper toward Sylvia. "That's Old Lau's address. I haven't seen her in ages, but she will tell you the truth and what to do. Please, you're the only one who can do something about the bridge. You aren't from around here. You haven't been changed. But, be careful. Most people don't want the bridge to be messed with, but I know those trapped spirits must move on. My poor Letitia must move on."

"I—"

"I'll call Old Lau and tell her you're coming—if she answers. She never answers anymore." Dave slammed the door.

Sylvia picked up the ball of paper, opened it, and looked at the address. The house was quiet, and she thought it best to leave.

"Thanks for your time," she said.

She got no reply.

* * *

Old Lau's address led Sylvia to a dilapidated cottage on the other side of town. Her senses told her she was in the right place, as if she needed to come here. It was an odd feeling to have, accompanied by a tingling sensation over her body. Hadn't Jimmy often said journalists develop an intuition when they're on the hot trail of a story? Yes, he had. She could remember fragments of those conversations, and she hoped he was right.

As she made her way across the yellowing lawn to the front door, she wondered why Old Lau hadn't solved the problem at the bridge, especially if she knew the truth and was intent on putting an end to its evil. Sylvia wasn't sure what she was really getting into, but she couldn't simply leave either. Added to her journalistic drive, there was some odd tether to the bridge. What if when people see something beyond what they know or understand of the world, they can't help but be drawn to it? Like a magnet.

Someone whistled at her before she reached the front door.

An elderly lady with deep-set narrow eyes and frizzled white hair sat in a wheelchair near the side of the house. It hit Sylvia like someone throwing book at her face: Old Lau must be Laura Mercy, the only person to have survived attempting to "commit suicide" at the bridge. How the fall hadn't killed her at her age, Sylvia wasn't sure. She racked her brain, trying to remember her notes, recalling Laura would be nearly seventy, though she looked to be in her mid-eighties.

"Took you long enough," Laura said.

"I'm sorry. You must have me mistaken for someone else. I'm Sylvia Bernstein, a reporter. Dave Daytona said you could tell me more about the bridge."

Laura's eyes narrowed. "Are you here to help?"

"I'll do what I can. Sharing the truth always brings anything wrong into the light."

"I see. Do you know who I am?"

"Yeah, you'd be Missus Laura Mercy?"

"Ha, sharp girl, ain't ya?" Laura turned her wheelchair. "Calling me Old Lau or jus' Laura will be fine. Now quick, follow me."

Sylvia trailed her down the side of the house, until Laura disappeared into a faded red shed.

"Close the door," Laura said after Sylvia entered. "Where were you born? You can't be leaving a door open like that."

Sylvia swung the creaky door closed. As soon as it clicked shut, Laura switched on a lamp next to her.

"You best take a seat, Sylvia. You have the look of someone who's seen them. No doubt you have questions," Laura said, playing with the ends of her hair. "You'll get your answers, but then you and I have some work to do. A mission."

Sylvia looked around the dusty shed and saw a wonky metal barstool. She pulled it nearer, clenching her teeth as it scraped on the hard, dirty floor.

"Good, good." Laura battled to straighten the fingers on her right hand, and Sylvia wondered if it was arthritis. "Jus' needs some warmth," Laura said, reaching into the side of her wheelchair. She pulled out a small flask. "Whiskey?"

Sylvia shook her head.

"I've been waiting for some help for a while. I can't pull it off by myself. No one else wants to help me, at least not anyone I trust."

"Dave?"

"Nah, he's too scared. He barely even leaves his house since, well, you know."

Sylvia nodded.

"Anyway, I'm just gonna tell you like it is. No bullshit." Laura took a sip from her flask. "The bridge is cursed, evil, or whatever else you want to call it. Most of those deaths, I'd say ninety-nine percent of them, barring the first one, weren't suicides. The first one, well, that may have been one, or it could've been some poor fool who fell. The first one, however, was the catalyst for the shit hitting the fan."

Laura took another sip, and then cleared her throat. "What I've found out is that when the bridge was made, they used pieces from a meteorite in its construction. By accident, or done by design, I'm not sure. Unfortunately, it came with disastrous consequences. I don't know where the hell the rock fell from, but it brought some weird stuff with it."

Sylvia shrugged. She had seen what she could only describe as ghosts or spirits. The idea it was some elaborate ruse had begun to dissolve. Seeing Laura, for some reason, only helped cement the realization of specters from beyond. Deep down she knew what she had seen was real, but the tale was taking an even stranger turn than what she'd expected. How far could the known reality stretch before the fabric tore and someone was flung out into space, or madness?

Laura looked at the flask but didn't take a sip. "So long story short, these pieces of meteorite in the bridge have somehow created a plane between the bridge and the ground below. And that's where these ghosts are stuck. They're only visible or active during dusk—I learned that the hard way. Bastards pulled me down one day. I'd stopped to check on my back tire when I felt something wrong with my vehicle. But, as you know, I survived the fall. Everyone in town kept to the same suicide story as all the others. They're scared or protective of the damn bridge. I followed along. Sure, I told a few people the truth, like Dave, but most could figure out what really happened. Anyway, like I said, they don't want to do anything. Having the dead around isn't natural. People shouldn't be near such a presence. There's a love-and-hate relationship with the bridge for most people who experience it. Like bugs attracted to a light, they can't seem to stay away, even if it's bad for them."

"That's crazy," Sylvia said. "I mean, if you'd told me all this before, I'd have thought you nuts, but I saw them, and the—"

"Touch," Laura said.

"Yeah, it was like death. Like real death."

"It is death," Laura said, dropping her gaze. "Guess we're both lucky to have survived."

"They left you? After you fell?"

"Must have. I was out. When I awoke, which could've been moments or a bit longer after the fall, it was night. Man, my chest and arms hurt like I'd been strung to the back of a horse and pulled throughout the entire Old West, but my legs, well, I didn't feel them. Next thing, I saw the police chief, and I blacked out again. I survived. That's all I know.

Laura wagged her finger up and down. "Oh, and listen, it's the chief and his buddy the priest who are the main culprits in the bridge being allowed to continue its unholy existence. We'll have to keep a watch out for those two."

Sylvia looked at Laura. The poor old woman was now in a wheelchair, unable to do anything about the bridge, while the town carried on the lie. This put more innocents at risk. Sylvia feared the ghosts, but a part of her was angry. She thought of Dave hiding away in his home. How many others had lost loved ones instead of putting an end to the evil?

"Okay, fuck it," she said. "How do we end this? How do I help you? Who do we call?"

"We call no one," Laura said, wheeling herself to a large black tarp. Grinning, she pulled it aside. There were crates packed full of dynamite.

"You must be kidding?" Sylvia asked.

"Nope."

"I don't think I really understand. Is that stuff even safe to be around?"

"It will have to be."

"For what?"

"We're going to blow up the cursed bridge."

* * *

Under the safety of night, Sylvia and Laura loaded Sylvia's car with the dynamite. Sylvia carried most of the dynamite, while Laura told her to "be careful, be careful." It took continuous persuasion from Laura to keep Sylvia on plan, but every time Sylvia thought of the touch, which was like an itch she couldn't scratch, her belief that Laura's way was best would be reignited.

They went over the plan a few times. It was a simple idea, but Sylvia didn't doubt Laura had been obsessing over it for ages. Sylvia also couldn't help but think of how many years she would spend in jail for this if they were caught. When Laura assured her no one would get hurt and that she would take the brunt of any trouble if things went south, Sylvia passed the point of no return.

During the ride, Sylvia grew apprehensive about returning to the bridge. This time the danger from the ghosts weighed on her mind. Laura promised more than once that when dusk had passed, it was safe. Her words proved to be true, as together they scouted the bridge upon arrival without any incident. Fortune also favored the two women, for during the whole time it took them to set up the dynamite, Sylvia never saw a single vehicle pass them.

Done setting up, which meant using every stick of dynamite, Sylvia left Laura at the town's side of the bridge. Here, Laura would hold a stop sign in case of any oncoming vehicles—a sign which had also been tucked away in her shed.

Sylvia drove to the other side of the bridge, and then a bit farther down the road. She parked her car in the middle of the road, trying to block as much of both lanes as possible. She jogged back to the bridge, took her flashlight, and signaled the all clear to Laura.

Laura signaled that the fuse had been lit.

"Shit, here we go," Sylvia said, retreating behind her car. Her heart rocked around in her chest like a rally driver in a roll cage tumbling down a hill.

Lights alerted Sylvia to an oncoming vehicle.

"What now?" she mumbled and marched into the middle of the road. She had to do something and hailed the car to halt; the driver obeyed, fortunately.

"What the hell are you doing?" the man asked, climbing out. "Stay in the car," Sylvia heard him say to the old male passenger.

Sylvia inhaled deeply, noticing the police emblem on the side of the vehicle. "I'm sorry, but there's a problem with the bridge."

"A problem? What problem? Who the hell are you? You're not from around here, are you? Let me guess: you're the one who was asking those questions at the gas station earlier today? You were the one out on the bridge earlier? You damn people never learn."

"Stay back."

"Stay back?" The man withdrew a firearm but kept it aimed at the ground. "I'm Police Chief Miller. Move away, or I arrest you."

"Just stay—"

Sylvia's world shuddered as a massive explosion echoed all around. Her ears rang so intensely she thought they were bleeding. Instinctively, she placed her hands over them and crouched forward. Miller shouted at her, but Sylvia only saw a mouth move. No sound arrived. She tried opening and closing her jaw.

The ringing faded, and the sounds of the world returned.

Miller asked, "Do you hear me? I asked what the fuck have you done?"

Sylvia flinched, fearful she was going to be shot or hit, but Miller's hardened expression changed. A look of concern draped over his visage now. He holstered his weapon and walked past her, toward the edge of the road that now ended in midair.

Their plan had worked. The bridge was gone. In its place rose a large black cloud. Faintness came over her as the ramifications of what they had accomplished solidified in her mind. Everything since the diner had happened so fast. She'd acted on impulse. The tether she had felt to the bridge since seeing it during dusk was gone. For some reason, the feeling of certainty in their plan weakened. Pulling herself together, she walked to Miller and stopped alongside him.

He gripped her shoulder and shook her violently. "What? What've you done?"

"I helped Laura destroy the bridge. What you people were doing here was wrong. I was at the bridge earlier. Its evil had to be stopped."

"Laura Mercy?"

"Yes."

"Interesting," Miller said, releasing her, "especially as she's been dead for some time."

Sylvia felt for her notebook, realizing she had left it in her vehicle. She did feel a lighter in one of her pockets, which she couldn't recall having. "No, she survived the fall."

"That's true," Miller said, nodding. "And then I shot her again."

"I don't understand."

"You don't realize what you've done. Laura's partner, Bill Simpson, was the first person to jump off the bridge. That was almost twenty years ago, and it wasn't simply suicide. They were leaders of some fucked-up cult. Bill wanted to open a portal, an evil portal. It almost worked, except—"

"No!" Sylvia shouted. "Laura told me they used meteorite rock when building the bridge. That's why a plane had been created—a plane where the dead got stuck."

Miller shook his head. "There was no meteorite rock. What kind of nonsense is that? It was the ritual he performed and then his sacrifice that was meant to open the intended portal, a portal that led to hell. He wanted to bring on the apocalypse. Father Clarkson, who's in the car, had warned me about their desires. We were ready for them. Father Clarkson used the bridge as a barrier to stop any demons getting through and foiled their plan. He drew signs and performed his own rituals, and we prayed a lot. It appeared to work, except that the pull remained even after we closed the portal. The plane is like an old scar."

Miller clenched his free hand into a fist. "Unfortunately, there've been people who got too close during the wrong time and got pulled in, only to be greeted by the hard ground. It's true that they're stuck between the realms of the living and the dead. And they come out during dusk. It's they who try and lure more people to share their fate, but that was a better alternative than an open portal."

"But, but," Sylvia said, raising her hands. Tears streaked her face. "She told me the bridge mustn't be."

"She disappeared after what happened to her husband, but I knew she wanted to finish their work. I spotted her a few times, cleaning scripture off of the bridge or removing amulets, but I never caught her, until one night. It was almost ten years ago, and she was trying to rig dynamite to the bridge. I told her that we'd long since put in other measures to close the portal for good, and destroying the bridge wouldn't get her what she wanted. I told her to stop, but she pulled a gun on me. I shot her, and then she, well, she jumped over."

Miller lowered his hand so that it rested above his pistol. "There used to be a path leading down, and by the time I got to the riverbed, she was crawling—still alive. Can you believe it? I told her it was over, but the evil bitch kept cursing me. So, I shot her again... I had to. I couldn't risk the town's safety. There were other things at stake. We—"

Sylvia put her hands over her face. "But if she's dead...how did I see her?"

"I guess when you came to the bridge earlier, she infected you somehow, and you ended up seeing some ghostly version of her in town. I can only assume she planted a seed so that you'd do her bidding while thinking you saw the real her, like a hallucination. You definitely didn't see the real physical version of her. Similar things have happened before, but this is the first time it worked this far. The town remains fucked even though we managed to permanently close the portal. While no legion of hell will come forth, all those spirits, people taken before their time, are now free. They've had to watch the townspeople enjoy life. Spirits should never linger. Only bad things come of that. We tried to keep people away without drawing too much outside attention to our problem, but the spirits still managed to lure the odd person in every now and again. All of them are full of hate and are intent on killing. They won't move on until they've exacted vengeance. Bill and Laura, especially, want to do harm. The rest of town will be their target."

"No! No!" Sylvia shouted, slapping Miller's chest. "There must be something we can do."

"Father Clarkson had been searching for a way to help the spirits move on peacefully. We were getting close. That no longer matters. As for the people, by the time we get around to the other entrance to town, it'll already be too late."

"Can't we call someone? The government? The army?"

"It's too—"

Screams burst into the air like air-raid sirens during a WWII bombing. Sylvia looked toward the town. Multiple houses were in flames, and black smoke reached into the heavens. Apart from the fire and screams, she couldn't tell what horror was going on throughout the community, but she could feel it. She thought of the man wearing the denim jacket at the diner, the staff there, and poor Dave. What atrocities befell them? The guilt ate away at her core like maggots feasting on the freshly dead.

Miller impersonated a statue as he gazed toward town. He would be no help. She turned and sprinted to the police vehicle. Father Clarkson had his Bible out and was reciting prayers with the speed of tongue to rival an auctioneer.

"Please, Father. You have to do something."

He looked up. His eyes widened as if he had seen the devil himself, but it wasn't Sylvia he focused on. "No, no, don't do it," he shouted at Miller.

Sylvia turned around.

Miller had his pistol out, aimed at his head. "I'm sorry, Father. I can't anymore."

He pulled the trigger.

THE TOWN THAT FEARED DUSK

A DINER AT THE END OF THE WORLD

The frustration gnawed at her innards like wolves picking on the bones of a kill, seeking the last scraps of flesh. How did grease always find its way onto the front counter? Tammy Washburn applied more force to battling the brown stain on the faded white surface. She would have moaned at Peyton Garcia, the diner's cook, had he been there, but she'd sent him and Ashley Tanner, a server, on an errand to get supplies. If they forgot the toilet paper, she might completely lose it.

There had been a change in their demeanors the last while. Were they itching to move on to other work? Ashley probably, but Peyton hadn't given off that vibe. Maybe it was the accident? Peyton had been driving one night, with Ashley as a passenger, when he'd struck Edith Venter, or Edith Goodhill as she had been known before marriage. She was a bustling elderly woman who worked as the head of the library. Edith had passed away due to the accident.

Maybe it was a combination of things that had affected Tammy's colleagues? Whatever it was, there was something up with them. Maybe she ought to give them the benefit of the doubt and cut them some slack?

She paused her attempts at cleaning the counter and inhaled deep. Why was she letting things get to her again? She had promised herself not to sweat the small stuff.

A cough came from across the room.

"You okay over there?" Tammy asked the only customer still in the diner. She hoped some cordial interaction would distract her.

Lloyd Reed, wearing a denim jacket, nodded.

Couldn't he say something interesting? Lloyd was one of the diner's regulars but barely spoke more than a few words. He ran his hand through his graying hair, clearing his throat before he placed his hand back on the counter. Lloyd enjoyed the three C's when seated at the diner: a coffee, a cigarette, and a crossword. Smoking was technically not allowed in the diner, but the rules were more relaxed when it was this late and empty. As if on cue, he reached into his pants pocket and pulled out a pack of smokes. He looked to Tammy, awaiting her approval.

Tammy nodded, then returned her focus to the door. Where were Peyton and Ashley? What on earth could be taking so long?

A loud *boom* startled her.

Two weaker *boom*s followed.

Lloyd stood, almost tripping on his chair's leg, and he hobbled toward the diner's front door, where he peered out into the dark world.

"You see anything?" Tammy asked, almost tiptoeing toward him.

He sighed, then shook his head.

"Wonder what that could've been? Maybe some kind of construction? Or a gas line? Maybe something electrical?"

"Hopefully one of those." Lloyd returned his gaze to his coffee. He appeared to be undecided whether he wanted to go and drink more of it or if he wanted to remain near the glass storefront of the diner.

"Should we go check what it is?"

Lloyd furrowed his brow. "Probably best to hang here a bit."

* * *

An engine roared as a red pickup pulled into the diner's parking lot, barely missing Tammy's own car. Lights illuminated the front of the vehicle as it stopped askew in one of the parking bays.

"Finally," Tammy said. "Peyton and Ashley are back. Maybe they'll know what those noises were."

Peyton stumbled out of his vehicle, but the passenger-side door never opened. By the time he grasped for the diner's front door, Tammy could already see the crimson liquid that stained his clothing. Some splatter had also found a home on his wild, unkempt beard. "What happened?" Tammy asked as he stepped into the diner. "Where's Ashley? Are you hurt?"

Peyton stumbled to the counter, where he stretched out his arms as if he were about to collapse. He didn't. Instead, he found his footing and turned back to face her and Lloyd. "I'm okay. It's not my blood. Ashley...didn't make it."

Lloyd stepped forward. "What do you mean?"

"We stopped so she could grab herself a soda...and...on the way out the store, well, this bluish circle of kinda smoke appeared and another blue thing, with like tentacles or something, reached out and...shit, it killed her. Blood went everywhere. I-I couldn't do fucking anything. I ran."

"What are you talking about?" Tammy asked. "You're in shock. You're not making any sense. Were you in another car accident?"

"Oh, he's making perfect sense." Lloyd turned to Tammy. "I think you know it, too."

"No. It can't be." Tammy placed her hand over her chest. "The bridge? It can't be."

Lloyd looked to Peyton. "Help me pull down the security gate."

"Wait," Tammy said. "What if people need to get in?"

"Pull the gate down now!"

Before Tammy could move, Peyton had already jumped into action. He yanked on the black gate, sending it banging against the floor. It bounced a little, and he steadied it, then lined up the gate to the latches. He proceeded to lock all the latches as Tammy stood puzzled.

"It can't be," she muttered. "It's been so long. Why now?"

"Peyton," Lloyd said, looking past Tammy, "let's move these chairs and tables to the front to be safe. And,

Tammy"—he returned his gaze to her—"switch off all the lights."

Tammy could sense the fear coursing through Lloyd; his face had hardened with dread. She didn't hesitate this time and bolted toward the light switches. There, she down pressed all of them as fast as possible with shaking hands. Had the town's shadowy history awoken? There had been so many rumors and stories interlaced with facts that it was hard to remember the exact warnings.

"Done," she said.

"Do we have any weapons?" Peyton asked.

Lloyd frowned. "Weapons won't help."

"Well, what can we do?"

"Wait it out and survive."

* * *

It didn't take long for the pandemonium to erupt, and with the diner being near the center of town, Tammy, Lloyd, and Peyton had a front-row seat to the chaos. Screams, gunshots, shouting, loud *bang*s, and other alarming noises sounded from all directions of town, but it wasn't until Mister Deeney—a teacher at the local school—trudged past the diner that the true horror of what unfolded was undeniable. The tall, thin man with curly grayish-brown hair was carrying his severed right arm. His pale face never glanced into the diner as he stumbled past, while blood dripped from the wound, leaving a trail of the splattered red substance on the concrete in his wake.

Tammy turned to Lloyd. "Should we—"

81

"No. He's on his own now."

What had happened to Mister Deeney? Tammy was too scared to dwell on the thought. He wouldn't get too far with the way he bled. That much, she was certain of. "Are you sure there's nothing we can do? What about trying to help some of the people? Maybe we can warn them?"

"Haven't you watched any horror films?" Peyton asked. "That's how you get killed."

"I'm afraid he's right," Lloyd said. "There's nothing we can do for anyone now. Hopefully, most of them have found places to hide out."

Banging on the diner's window ended their conversation. Tammy attempted to peer out from one of the tables she had ducked behind. Was Mister Deeney back? An image of him banging his severed arm on the window popped up in her mind. Fortunately, that wasn't the case, as two middle-aged women—Martha and Louise—stood at the front of the diner. The two of them ran a small clothing store up the road.

Martha banged on the window again. "Hey, is anyone in there? We need help. There are injured people."

"Don't let them know we're here," Lloyd said from his hiding spot next to the diner's counter.

Tammy thought Peyton might leap up to help his fellow townsfolk, or maybe she wanted him to, but he didn't. They deserved help, but she didn't want to be the one who brought forth any adverse consequences if she aided them.

"Hello?" Martha said, banging away again.

Louise seemed odd. Tammy surveyed her intently while trying not to reveal herself. Blood had stained Louise's floral top, and she held her hands in tight-clenched fists. Her pale face revealed no emotion. Something wasn't right. Maybe Lloyd had been correct in wanting the three of them to remain hidden in the diner?

Martha moved off; Louise followed her sluggishly.

Tammy considered that it might be best to listen to Lloyd for the remainder of the night. He knew more than the usual stories regarding the bridge and its hold over their town.

* * *

A figure appeared from out of the night. The young man stopped right in front of the diner's front door. He had no injuries—in fact, he looked healthy, and his clothes were clean and neat. Tammy stared at his face. It couldn't be, but it was. The young man was family of hers: her nephew.

Tammy said, "Do you guys see—"

"The young man standing in front?" Lloyd said. "Yeah, we see him. Did he pass away? Did you know him?"

"Yeah, he was my nephew. How did you know he passed?"

"Just a feeling."

"How did he find his way here? He didn't die here. I mean...I assume that he saw the bridge for him to do what he did. I tried to warn him. I should never have mentioned the place to him."

"You never leave the bridge once it gets its hooks in you. It's haunted my family for ages. You know of my grandfather?"

"Yeah. I've heard a story or two."

"Most people think a guy named Bill Simpson might've been the first to die at the bridge. That isn't true. That place's history is way darker and older than anyone remembers, except maybe for a few."

"Do you know the history?"

"Only as far back as my grandfather uncovered before the bridge got him."

Tammy's nephew must have grown tired of staring blankly at the diner, as he turned around and headed across the street. A faint blue cloud emanated from him as he walked away, like a shadow that wasn't relegated to surfaces.

"How are we going to escape? Can we escape?" Tammy asked.

"We have to wait until morning," Lloyd said. "The town will never be the same, but that will be the best chance to escape."

"Leave Goohill, forever?"

"You're welcome to stay, but I have had my fill of this place. I should've left many years ago, but some people in town felt sorry about what happened to my family, especially those who didn't help my grandfather when it still could've truly made a difference. They offered me good work."

"I'm out of here first chance I get," Peyton said. "I only rent and nothing at home is worth my life." Even though Lloyd had told him weapons wouldn't help, he'd already procured a large knife from the kitchen as well as a hefty piece of wood that he clearly intended to use as a club or baseball bat.

"I rent as well," Tammy said. "I guess I don't have much I couldn't replace. Maybe some photos, oh, and an old kitchen set my aunt gave me."

"Well, I own a place, and it's full of antiques I inherited," Lloyd said, "but I'm not dying for it."

The night continued with intermittent screams, *bangs*, crashes, shouting, and various other noises of chaos. Figures, shapes, and people came and went as well, seemingly oblivious to the three of them in the diner.

"Do you really think we'll be safe in here?" Tammy asked Lloyd.

"Yeah. The first night will likely see the easy victims getting targeted."

Tammy nodded, then beheld the diner's front.

Her nephew had returned.

This time, he had brought along a friend. The old man wearing a navy-blue baseball cap stood alongside him. Both stared vacantly into the diner with faint blue light emanating from their eyes. Their facial expressions never changed, nor did their bodies move as they stood, imitating statues.

"Who is the other guy?" Peyton whispered.

"My grandfather," Lloyd said. "Ivan Reed."

"The one the bridge got?"

"Yup. He died many, many years ago."

* * *

The sun did rise again. Both Tammy's nephew and Lloyd's grandfather had vacated their post before its arrival. Had Lloyd been correct? Would they have a moment to escape? The cacophony of unnerving sounds had also ceased, and now, silence reigned while a faint smell of smoke hung in the air.

"Time to go." Lloyd marched to the front of the diner.

Peyton didn't waste a second and jumped up to follow him. Tammy felt anxiety flood her, but she willed movement upon herself and stood. Focusing on one step after the other, she reached the front of the diner.

Outside, she surveyed the world. A vehicle in the distance to her right was burning, while a pickup to her left lay upside down—none of their vehicles in the diner's parking area had been damaged. She exhaled slowly, audibly. A couple of the other storefronts had shattered or broken windows; smoke billowed in the sky from two spots in town farther away. Were they homes? Were they buildings? She wasn't sure.

Blood had splattered all over the concrete beneath her, and the dark crimson fluid also covered the white door of a building across the road from them. A bloodied shoe lay in the middle of the road before them, but it wasn't the only clothing item she noticed, as a torn T-shirt hung on a pole a few feet to her left. There were no bodies.

"Madness," she muttered.

"Yeah," Peyton replied.

A black car came speeding down the road before them. The driver, a middle-aged or older man, paid no attention to the three of them standing outside the diner, as his focus was solely on the road ahead. He barely avoided the overturned pickup as the roar of his car's engine echoed in the silence of town. Clear of the obstacle, he sped away into the distance.

"Who was that?" Peyton asked.

"I think it was Father Clarkson," Tammy said.

"Hell," Lloyd said, "if the town's main priest is running, it's time we all do the same."

Lloyd climbed into his vehicle. Peyton and Tammy didn't waste any time in climbing into theirs. They started their engines and followed him out of the diner's parking area and onto the road.

* * *

Unlike Father Clarkson, they headed for the bridge. It was the quickest way out of town. They had discussed their exit route during the previous night and concluded it was best to aim for the fastest escape. Tammy and Peyton had pondered what might await them, but Lloyd had felt sure that whatever ritual might have taken place at the bridge, those responsible would've cleared out by now, at least until the evening. Even though he had been correct all night, Tammy couldn't stop imagining a mass of people huddled at the bridge, waiting for them. She had considered attempting to overrule Lloyd, but Peyton had caved and ceded to him before she could muster enough courage to speak out—two against one. Why take the risk? That's what she should've asked. She had contemplated going on her own and taking the other exit from town, but the thought of being alone until clear of this hellish place frightened her. She had eventually decided she would follow them out, but she would do so on her own terms: keeping a safe distance from the two of them just in case.

As they drove through the town, the world mimicked the destruction they had seen outside the diner. Vehicles with broken windows abandoned in the middle of the road became perpetual obstacles for them. There was even an abandoned stroller in one street, while the expected dirty, torn, and blood-spattered clothing littered the neighborhoods in various spots. A few small fires still burned in areas. Fortunately, none appeared to be spreading. There was no sign of any fire department, police, or ambulances. Apart from Father Clarkson, Tammy hadn't seen another soul. Had most of them escaped? Were some of them still hiding?

As they entered the stretch of road leading to the bridge, the abandoned vehicles became much fewer, making life easier. Lloyd and Peyton both accelerated due to the lack of obstacles. Tammy followed their lead. A brief flame of hope flickered within her, but she couldn't resist moving over a tad to the left. She wanted clear sight of the bridge. The idea of seeing it before it saw her had popped into her mind.

A road sign, indicating how far the next two towns were, appeared up ahead. Something was wrong. The bridge should have been visible by now. She intended to honk, but paused, realizing Lloyd and Peyton had increased their speed. What the hell were they doing? She looked ahead, hoping the bridge would come into view. It didn't. Lloyd and Peyton were speeding toward...nothing. It hit her like a slap to the face on a cold winter's day, there was no bridge. The *booms* had been explosions. Someone had destroyed the bridge.

She attempted to remove her foot from the accelerator and hit the brakes before bashing her horn, except her foot felt as if it had been encased in a concrete block. She couldn't move it. Her arms remained hardened, with her hands clenched onto the steering wheel, headed straight for the newly created fall. An urge rose within, wanting her to accelerate and surrender to the void.

She resisted.

Up ahead, Lloyd's vehicle disappeared and then Peyton's pickup vanished as well. Two loud *bangs* followed their disappearance. Tammy had to do more than resisting, or she would share their fate. She mustered all her might, managing to lift her foot on the accelerator, while bringing her other foot down on the brakes. Whatever force battled her was potent and growing stronger with every moment. She had to do something unexpected, something crazy. Bracing herself for impact, she yanked down hard on the steering wheel, fighting her own body's resistance.

The vehicle turned and then flipped over.

A bright whiteness exploded in Tammy's view.

* * *

A miracle? Maybe it had been. Tammy opened her eyes and found herself curled up in her vehicle, which was lying on its roof. She climbed out of the wreckage, thankful that the door opened without any problems, but expecting serious pains to explode over numerous spots on her body. They didn't, as apart from a few minor cuts and bruises, she was okay.

Outside the vehicle, she had a decision to make. Walk toward the demolished bridge—which was barely a stone's throw away from her now—or not? She wanted to see if Lloyd or Peyton had survived, but a barrage of questions brought conflicting emotions. What if one of them had survived but needed serious assistance? What if going nearer to the bridge brought back the force she had felt?

Fear won.

Tammy turned her back to the void; except she didn't walk. They'd helped her survive the night, and she had to at least do something for them. She decided to count until sixty, to wait and see if she heard any cries for help or screams from either of them.

None came.

Tammy considered their speed plus the fall, concluding there was almost no hope of survival. She searched for more thoughts to console herself that she was making the best decision in a dire situation. A different track of thoughts took hold. Maybe having avoided the bridge most of her life had saved her? Lloyd and Peyton had likely succumbed to the intrigue of the bridge over the years and had visited it, as so many people eventually did. She hadn't. Apart from driving over it when there was no other option, she had never stepped a foot on its surface. What had Lloyd said? *You never leave the bridge once it gets its hooks in you.* Maybe the force pulling on them had been more potent than for her due to their previous interactions with the bridge. There was nothing she could have done for them.

She lumbered toward town, ignoring the pain in her ankle as best as possible, while contemplating her options. Could she make it all the way through town and reach the other road exiting the cursed place? The fear of what could be waiting, watching surfaced.

The hum of an engine broke the silence.

A blue pickup approached.

Who could it be? She wished it were some kind of authority, preferably the police coming to her rescue. If it was a local, there was a good chance she would recognize them. Maybe they would offer her a lift out of this place? The potency of the old bridge and what had happened to Lloyd and Peyton entered her thoughts, and she ran toward the vehicle, waving her arms, hoping they would stop before they got too close, while ignoring the rising pain in her ankle.

The blue pickup stopped.

A man wearing long gray pajamas and navy-blue slippers climbed out.

"Dave Daytona? I heard you never left the house."

"That's not true at all. I leave when I need stuff. I'm just careful about when not to be out, unlike most of you."

"Okay, okay, relax. Listen, you can't get too close to the bridge... Well, what's left of it."

"I know. I just wanted to see what had happened here. I had a feeling something like this might occur."

"What do you mean?"

"It's not important. What are you doing here? I thought you might be one of them for a moment."

"It's not important. I need a ride out of this town. We can't stay here. Whatever is happening is going to get worse."

Dave nodded while glancing around, almost as if he was seeking someone. Tammy remembered he had a daughter. Was it Lucy, Letitia, or Lesley? She couldn't recall, but it was something like that. Hadn't she committed suicide at the bridge? Tammy thought of asking Dave but ceased the idea immediately. People were on edge after what happened the previous night, and she didn't want to tip the scales one way or the other.

Tammy hurried to the passenger-side door. "Come on, let's get going."

"Yeah," Dave said, climbing into the vehicle.

"Is this yours?" Tammy asked as Dave started the engine. "I didn't know you still drove."

"It's not mine. It belongs to Walter Deeney. He's a teacher at—"

"Yeah, I know him."

"Right. Anyway, I found it abandoned in the street a few houses down from my place. Keys were in it, and the door was wide open. I didn't think he'd mind me borrowing it, considering all that's going on."

Tammy nodded.

"Do you need to stop anywhere?"

"No," Tammy said. "Let's just get out of this fucking town."

THE TOWN THAT FEARED DUSK

FROM DUSK TILL DEATH

Today didn't exist.

It couldn't.

A permanent marker had blacked it out on the calendar.

Barry Clarkson raised his head above the blanket, focusing on the blur that was his glasses, which sat on the bedside table next to him. The room's curtains were drawn, and shades of gray colored his surroundings; he guessed it must be early evening. He put his large-framed glasses on and searched for certain objects.

The rabbit's foot, on the bedside table, was easy to find. The large cross on the wall to his left came next, and it hung nice and straight. Following that was the horseshoe, pointing up and hanging on the wall to his right.

Barry looked above his head.

The dreamcatcher was there.

He turned his head, concentrating hard: the acorn rested on the windowsill on the opposite side of the room. For the last object, he felt underneath his pillow. The most important object was where it should be.

"Good, good," he mumbled, cradling the item in his hand.

He sought the bedside table for his glass of water, which was the reason for the unscheduled wake-up. His plan had been to sleep away most of the day that could not be, but his parched throat had betrayed him, as it had earlier that morning when he'd briefly awoken to have some water and a stale cereal bar. He gripped the glass, but wrinkled hands shaking from many years of use couldn't hold it properly.

The glass tipped over.

Before Barry could grab it, it fell to the floor, and he ducked back under his blanket. He shook his head. Though a falling glass wasn't on his ultimate red-alert list, Barry didn't like the possible chain reactions it could set off.

A knock at the door disrupted his thoughts; the door handle rattled.

Who would be disturbing him today? One name caused Barry to shiver beneath the blanket.

The door creaked open.

"Barry, what is this nonsense I hear? You told Gwen that you weren't to be disturbed today. This isn't a hotel."

His nightmare had come true. He couldn't imagine a worse day to run afoul of her.

"Get out from under that blanket. You're seventy-odd, not five."

Barry raised his head above the blanket.

Margaret Anne Frost was standing in the doorway, a frown on her face as she held a brown paper bag. She was a short, thin lady who had quite the eccentric dress sense. Today she wore a white dress with an array of colorful flowers, while brown boots found home over her feet, and to top off her look she had draped a bright red scarf around her neck. Margaret ran the old-age home where Barry stayed, though she dabbled in many other duties, from nurse to psychiatrist and sometimes disciplinarian—her favorite.

Barry liked all the other employees of the home, just not her. She was uncaring, dismissive, and quick to anger. He decided to behave, hoping it would see her leave him be.

"Good evening, Miss Frost."

"Barry, get your wrinkly old ass out of bed. You're going to miss supper."

Barry frowned. If only he could buy time, maybe Margaret would get bored and go and disturb someone else. "Yes, Miss Frost. I'll need to change first. I'm still in my pajamas."

"There's no time." Margaret tapped her foot, placing her hand on her hip. "Come now, Barry. You'll have to go as is. Let this serve as a reminder for your childish nonsense. Never in my life have I heard someone so scared of Friday the—"

"Don't say it," Barry blurted out.

"Friday the thirteenth. Friday the thirteenth," Margaret said. "Should I say it some more or are you coming?"

Barry's world shuddered, but he managed to throw his skinny legs over the side of the bed. "I'm coming. Please stop saying it." He looked at his long blue pajama pants, which he wore inside out like all his clothes—when he could get away with it.

Hoping supper would be over soon, he stumbled forward, contemplating ways to sneak back into his room without anyone noticing and before anything terrible happened.

* * *

Sleight of hand had seen Barry sneak the object from under his pillow into his pants pocket, and even though he gripped it tight, an uneasy feeling rumbled in his core. Margaret had never worried about him missing supper before, as that would be the duty of someone below her. His concern upgraded to fear when she attempted to lead him past the eating area's entrance, and Barry came to a halt.

"Come on, Barry," Margaret said.

"But why aren't we going in?" Barry peered into the large room. He could see a few people still seated enjoying their meals.

"We're going to eat outside."

"Outside?"

"Yes, outside. You ate supper outside yesterday, and you even sat by one of the tables playing chess with William afterward."

"But not today, not on the bad day."

Margaret gripped Barry's forearm tight. "Now listen to me. Some of your nonsense has infected the more gullible residents here. I can't have that." She paused and smiled as one of the other employees, Ruth, walked by.

98

"By getting you outside today," Margaret continued, "I'll make everyone see all the nonsense you spout is just that: nonsense. I'm tired of hearing all these stories you tell, especially the one about the bridge. I know more about you than you think."

Barry noticed something dangling from Margaret's scarf.

Instinctively, he reached for it.

Margaret, watching where his hand was going, intercepted him and pulled off the tag. She held it in front of Barry. "Nine dollars and ninety-nine cents. Quite a score for such a beautiful scarf, no?"

Barry flinched as he saw the numbers, because Margaret held the tag upside down and instead of seeing the bargain price, all Barry had seen was 6-6-6. He tried to regain composure and mumbled, "Yes, a great deal, Miss Frost."

Surely it was pure coincidence. Barry attempted to brush off yet another ominous sign. Are there really coincidences, though?

"Anyway," Margaret said, crumpling up the tag, "once everyone sees all your mumbo jumbo is ridiculous, things can go back to normal."

"It's not nonsense. I can even show you in some of the books and newspapers—"

"About that stuff, I think it's time we're a bit stricter on what we allow to circulate within these walls."

Barry wanted to argue against this, but Margaret pulled on his arm.

Reluctantly, he followed her. His breathing had quickened, and shorter breaths made him confused, but he fought for clear thoughts. If he could survive a few moments outside, hopefully, she would allow him back to the sanctuary of his room.

* * *

They carried on through one of the halls leading outside, and Barry had almost managed to find a workable equilibrium when he saw it. Standing directly in front of the open glass door that exited into the front yard was an open ladder.

A young man with curly brown hair, whom Barry recognized as Richard's son, Mark, stood before the ladder. Richard was the local handyman, and Barry concluded that must be why the ladder stood there; repair work or painting or something of the sort was in progress. Mark gave his father a hand with some of the jobs.

Mark exited, simply ducking under the ladder, straightening up, and then carrying on along the stone pathway outside.

Barry had wanted to shout to him but found that he couldn't speak or move. Did Mark not understand what he'd done? You can't walk under a ladder without repercussions. The world distorted, and objects seemed to blend into each other. A dark thought brewed within: was this some evil trick that Margaret had schemed up?

Realizing he had stopped a few feet from the exit, Barry wanted to turn and flee, but all he could manage was to raise his arm and point at the ladder. He wouldn't be going any farther. Margaret hadn't noticed—she'd already exited the building, ducking under the ladder as Mark had done.

She turned around. "Come on now, Barry. I haven't got all evening. There are important matters for me to attend to."

All the things Barry had read about ladders rushed through his head. "Do not break the triangle. Do not break the triangle," he mumbled as Margaret continued talking, but somehow her words had become unintelligible, almost as if they were another language. He focused and slowly the world around him returned to normal.

"Mark, can you please take this damn ladder?" Margaret asked. "I told you to put it away after you were done with the work for the day."

Mark jumped back into view and moved the ladder outside. It wobbled a bit as it got accustomed to its new spot. "I'm almost done, Miss Frost. I just need to do one or two quick checks before my dad gets back."

Margaret looked back at Barry. "You happy now?"

Barry nodded, though he couldn't resist and knocked on a wooden counter as he made his way outside. Margaret simply shook her head in pity. When they walked down the pathway, he managed to say, "You went under the ladder."

Margaret chuckled. "See, I told you all that stuff is rubbish."

* * *

They sat on one of the wooden benches on the front lawn. The clement weather of the last few days was turning, and a chill rode the air as dusk arrived. Margaret lifted the bag she had been carrying onto the table. She took out a plastic container holding sandwiches, then handed one to Barry. She reached back into the bag and revealed two orange juices.

After offering Barry a juice, she dug into her sandwich.

Barry did the same and was about to take another bite of the chicken-and-mayo sandwich when he heard Margaret's bone-chilling chuckle again.

"Ah," Margaret said, "a few minutes of them seeing you out here, on Friday the thirteenth of all days, and all this superstitious nonsense will be over."

Barry's heart skipped a beat at the mention of the date, but he pushed past the feelings. He looked around; Margaret had been right about people being curious to find him out today. Many of the other residents wandered around them. Some were alone, looking confused, while others walked in groups, whispering.

"Well, Barry. You might as well entertain me." Margaret picked at her teeth. "I hear you say you saw ghosts by some haunted bridge. Weren't you still a priest back then? You must have snapped and had some fall from grace, huh?"

"What happened was real. I don't care about the cover—"

"Contaminated water. Isn't that what they said happened? It killed half the town and made the other half nuts. I heard some people told the most bizarre tales until the government stepped in and sorted things out." Margaret shook her head. "Terrible. Did they figure out what caused it? Maybe it was some company polluting. You could all sue if it was."

"It wasn't water contamination."

"Hmm... But even the bridge story doesn't explain all your other...things."

Barry knew what she alluded to. He had tried to explain all the objects he kept and the rituals he practiced to other members of the staff. It never did any good, as they would only nod along, smile, or pretend to care as if they were merely indulging the fantasies of a misguided old man.

"Come on, Barry. Explain all the other stuff. I heard you have a rabbit's foot and that you hop over cracks on the pavement."

"I want good luck. Is that so bad?" Barry asked.

It was more than wanting good luck, though. It was about the nightmares from the bridge, seeing evil, seeing darkness from the realms beyond. Anything Barry could do to stave off forces of darkness was important to him.

Margaret had been correct about him being a priest in that godforsaken town. He'd known the bridge was evil there after a couple from a cult had performed a failed ritual to open a portal to hell. He'd done all he could to protect the town, but when a young reporter, influenced by evil, decided to blow up the bridge, all the people who had died committing suicide at the bridge—

and there were many—were free to cause havoc on the town before moving on.

After the disaster of that night, he had relinquished his position and attempted to tell his side of the story. No one had believed him. He ended up in an institute or two before landing here at the old-age home.

"What's your most important possession, then?" Margaret asked.

"The dreamcatcher above my bed," Barry lied.

He couldn't tell her that his most important possession was in his pants pocket. The urge to hold it came, but he didn't, as he couldn't let Margaret catch on to him having it on him. The object was a piece of the bridge that he had found among the rubble. It had scripture, which he'd written on the bridge after the couple's failed ritual, perfectly preserved. At the time, he debated taking the piece of stone, but it proved to be a good call as with the evil leaving, the stone now brought him good luck and the scripture continued its purpose of keeping the darkness away.

As time went on, he focused on other items and rituals that could help fend off the darkness or at least keep it at bay. Once he had seen the true evil of the other side, he'd do everything to never have to encounter it again. A lot of people said he had suffered a serious psychological break after what they lied and called "the water contamination disaster," but Barry knew better.

"A dreamcatcher. How interesting," Margaret said, even though her face revealed disappointment. Maybe she had wished it were something more dangerous? Something she could easily confiscate.

Done eating, Margaret collected all their rubbish and made her way to a large bin a few feet from them. She chucked all the rubbish in, clapped her hands together, and made her way back.

Barry watched with ever-widening eyes as she stopped and kicked at the ground. He dropped his gaze, trying to see what she was doing.

Before he could say anything, she brought one of her boots down upon a spider about the size of a casino chip.

Barry flinched as she raised her foot.

"Haha, got him," Margaret said.

Barry shook his head. Everything was wrong. He couldn't gloss over the signs any longer; he should never have left his room, even if that had meant throwing a fit. He hoped Margaret was done with him and that he could finally be left alone.

Something soft hit the top of his head.

Around him, people hustled to get indoors.

"Come on, Barry. I've proven my point. Let's get inside before you start doing some crazy dance to stop the rain," Margaret said, waving her hands in front of her, then pulling a funny face with narrowed eyes and her tongue sticking out the corner of her mouth.

"No, you do the dance for rain. I think it might have started raining because you stood on—"

"Shut up."

Barry kept quiet. Margaret's cheeks had begun to redden. The scowl that appeared over her face wasn't one to mess with.

"Not another damn word about any superstitions, ghosts, or bridges. Or I swear I'll take away all possessions and privileges. I will punish you like no one has been punished before. Are we clear?"

"Uh-huh."

"I said, are we clear?"

"Yes, Miss Frost. We're clear."

"Now smile and follow me. We're heading in."

* * *

Every atom in Barry's being yearned to return to his room as he followed Margaret. He didn't care that this had been some ploy on her part to get all the residents to lose belief in his superstitions. He had only offered them advice. It was for them to decide what they believed.

As they approached the glass sliding door leading back into the building, he could see some of the residents lined up inside, watching. Some shook their heads at him, and others had long sullen faces. His speed decreased; he couldn't help but feel their disappointment.

"Barry, walk faster," Margaret said. "You're gonna be drenched and I don't want to be paying the cost for your medicines if you catch a cold from tardiness."

Barry was about to obey when a coin on the ground caught his eye. Crouching for a closer inspection, he couldn't believe what he saw—it was a penny, a real

British penny. Did it belong to William? William Wilshire was the old-age home's top coin-and-stamp collector. As he picked up the coin, he made a mental note to show it to William. Finding a penny was good luck. Had the day finally taken a turn for the better?

Placing the coin in his pocket, Barry heard a loud crash, followed by a deep cracking sound right by him. He jumped back to a standing stance with youth-like reflexes and looked around for Margaret, but she was gone. He lowered his gaze, a chill shooting down his spine.

The ladder that had been standing before the door earlier now lay on top of an inert Margaret.

A large pool of blood formed around her body.

"Shit, shit," Mark said, getting up.

"What happened?" Barry asked.

Mark, with widened eyes and pale cheeks, hobbled toward Margaret. "The damn rain, man. I was on the ladder checking on one of the gutters when I slipped. I knew I was going to fall. I didn't know anyone was behind me."

He knelt alongside Margaret. "Miss Frost. Miss Frost... Are you okay? Please move."

He checked her pulse. "I-I think she-she's dead. Bu-but it was just a ladder. I-I..."

The word *dead* brought lucid thought, and Barry forgot about the penny and reached into his opposite pants pocket for the piece from the bridge. Had it protected him? He could easily have been him lying there and not Margaret. He held the piece of bridge firm and moved past Mark, noticing how much darker his surroundings were; night was taking over.

As he entered the building, the residents who had been watching were all in hysterics. They kept pushing toward him, asking him what had happened and if Margaret was all right. It wasn't until Ellen—the notorious gossip queen of the home—stepped forward, her silver hair cascading to her shoulders, that Barry was able to speak.

"Shh, shh, everyone. Barry, is Margaret all right? What happened?" Ellen asked.

Barry shook his head. "I told her today was bad, but she wouldn't listen. The signs were everywhere. She...she's dead."

"Oh no."

People all around gasped at the news; some huddled together, while others couldn't resist wrapping arms around one another.

"Are you okay, Barry?" Ellen asked, stroking his forearm.

"Yeah, a penny on the ground saved me. I really just want to get to my room. Today is a bad day."

"Of course, Barry. You go ahead."

"Wait," a voice said.

Another of the residents, Sophia, with her large, soft green eyes, stepped toward Barry. She passed him a necklace, which he took and then held up so he could see what dangled on it.

"It's a charm: a four-leaf clover," Sophia said. "I'm also wearing one and can make them for others who need them. I've ordered all sorts of charms. Did I do right?"

"Yes." Barry smiled.

"That's lovely, Sophia," Ellen said. She looked back at Barry. "You go on to your room, Barry. We have everything under control now. We'll see you tomorrow, when the bad day has passed."

Barry nodded and walked away.

The crowd parted for him.

All of the residents watched him intently; some gently patted his arms and shoulders as he walked by. Most of them seemed to have momentarily forgotten about Margaret. He heard them ask each other multiple questions. *What should we do? What should we wear? What other objects can I get for good luck?* were but a few.

As he entered the corridor leading back to his room, he could hear Ellen's booming voice.

"All right, everyone. You heard what Barry said. Today is the bad day. It has been proven. Let us all head back to our rooms until tomorrow. And to those who have them, remember to hang up your dreamcatchers and horseshoes along with the crosses most of you already have on your walls. Tomorrow, when Barry is feeling better, we'll find out what else we can do."

Sadness weighed over Barry as if he were a coffin with a fresh mound of dirt covering it. Margaret hadn't deserved such a gruesome death. Yet she had chosen to ignore all the signs. A tinge of happiness fought and grew stronger inside of him, like a plant energized by the sun, with the realization that the other residents were beginning to protect themselves.

He entered his room, closed the door, and climbed into bed.

He did a check on all the objects in the room.

Satisfied, he placed the piece of the bridge under his pillow and rested his heavy head down. He pulled his blanket over himself and slept away what remained of the day that should not be.

NOW LEAVING GOOHILL

Relief washed over you as you saw the sign that read *Now Leaving Goohill.* You had stopped at a gas station before town, thinking that you might pop in at a local diner to grab a bite to eat, but anxiety had grown within ever since you entered Goohill. The employee at the gas station was frigid, appearing like a statue until you engaged them, but even then, their replies had been monosyllabic. When you mentioned the town, they had gone mute, and they'd remained that way until you left their premises.

A chill had penetrated your vehicle as you drove down the main street of the small town. Shadows fell unnaturally over the world outside as tones of gray crept in, sending the sun's last rays of light into retreat. No, it would be better to push through. You ignored your stomach's groan. You glanced at the small businesses lining the street, hoping they would take your mind off the ever-growing sense of unease. They didn't. If anything, their aged, callous exteriors only added more butterflies to the kaleidoscope fluttering in your stomach. Wasn't it funny how some old buildings had charm, history, and warmth, while others only had a stale coldness, or worse: nightmares?

As you exited the town, houses gave way to open fields with sporadic spots of trees with hills in the far distance. You thought you were free, but a police cruiser appeared in the rearview mirror. The cruiser came up alongside you, and a young officer indicated for you to pull over. What now? Why this? What could you do? You hadn't done anything wrong.

You wanted to slam the accelerator down.

You regretted visiting family in this part of the country.

Instead, you pulled off the road and rolled down your window, waiting to see what the officer wanted. You knew there was nothing wrong with the vehicle and you hadn't been speeding.

"Hi. I'm Officer Miller," the man said as he stood next to your vehicle.

"Hi. How can I help you, Officer?"

"You're not from around here? I don't recognize you."

"No, I'm not."

Officer Miller tapped the badge on his chest. "I recently graduated."

"Congrats."

A smile stretched across his face. "Thank you. I got transferred here, like a month back."

"Why would you want to be transferred to such a small town?" You couldn't resist asking the question, before realizing that Officer Miller probably didn't have much choice in where they stationed him.

"Oh, I wanted to be here. I grew up here. My uncle used to be police chief of this fine town. Goohill is such a unique place, and it has this special draw, you know? I think my uncle would've been happy to see me follow in his footsteps." Officer Miller dropped his gaze.

"I'm sure he would. It's great that you were able to get placed somewhere you wanted to be."

"Yeah. You just passing through?"

"Yup. Just passing through."

"Mind me asking what you're doing in the area?"

"Visiting family."

"Oh, I see. This your ride?"

"A rental. I've got all my documentation here if you need it."

"Oh, no, no," Officer Miller said, taking a step back. "I was only making conversation."

"Then why'd you stop me?"

"Ah..." Officer Miller looked around. "Just trying to be friendly."

You didn't believe him, but it didn't matter. Your only concern was hitting the road again. "Am I free to go?"

An elderly woman in a wheelchair appeared from a group of bushes to your left. She had deep-set, narrow eyes and frizzled white hair. The woman struggled to get onto the road. Officer Miller, instead of helping, mumbled a curse word and shook his head at her arrival. Once on the road, the woman moved much easier and headed straight for you both.

"What are you doing here?" Officer Miller asked her. "We don't have time for your nonsense today."

The old woman ignored him. Instead, she looked directly at you. "Are you a reporter? I need a fellow colleague. We must go back to town and document all the evil."

You were puzzled, but answered, "I'm—"

"Let me in the car! We need to go back to town. There is evil everywhere. It's a cursed place. I need your help to document the evil."

"I'm sorry. I'm strapped for time."

The woman rounded the vehicle and attempted to open the passenger-side door. Once she realized you had locked it, she banged on the passenger window. "Open up. We need to document—"

Officer Miller pushed the old woman's wheelchair away from the vehicle.

"Let me go, you bastard!"

"I've had enough of your baloney," Officer Miller said. "I'm taking you in for interfering in my duties."

The woman tried to bite his right hand.

He flinched in time. "Stop your shit, or I'll have you for attacking an officer as well."

Officer Miller pushed her toward his cruiser. There, he placed her in the back seat, and after a minute or two managed to get her wheelchair in his trunk. You watched the entire episode unfold. Time slowed, and you questioned if you had driven into an alternate reality. Maybe you should have driven away? The officer clearly hadn't stopped you for any official reason.

Officer Miller marched back to you. "I'm sorry you had to see all that."

"Is she okay?"

"Not really. Well, she used to be, apparently, but then she had a mental break many, many years ago. Now, she kind of terrorizes the town, especially any newcomers. She's into a lot of that conspiracy garbage."

"Oh, I see. That's terrible. She getting any help?"

"I think people in town have tried to sort her out, but she just keeps reappearing."

"What's her name?"

"Ah..." Officer Miller glanced back at his cruiser. "Everyone calls her Old Sylvie."

"What did she used to do? Before her break?" You knew you should've let it be, but the intrigue sent the question spurting from your lips before better judgment could rein you in. Everything was off about this place, even the people, and especially their stories.

Officer Miller shrugged. "I've kept you for far too long. Hope you have a safe trip, and thanks for visiting our little town."

You smiled as best you could, realizing he never added the usual "come again," as people do. Relief, however, washed over you as you started your vehicle. As you pulled away, leaving Officer Miller and Old Sylvie in your wake, you almost felt like yourself again.

You pledged to never come this way in the future.

Goohill wasn't a place for you.

www.ingramcontent.com/pod-product-compliance
Lightning Source LLC
Chambersburg PA
CBHW031254210726

48287CB00003B/1027